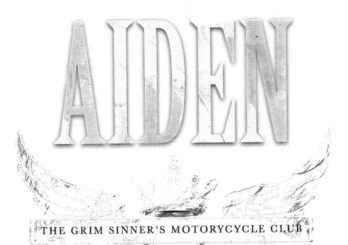

AIDEN

THE GRIM SINNER'S MOTORYCYCLE CLUB

LeAnn Ashers

COPYRIGHT

Designer: Regina Wamba

Photographer: Wander Aquilar

Editor: Stephanie Marshall Ward at Eats, Shoots, Edits

Formatter: Small Town Girl Formatting

DEDICATION

*This is for all those who thought they couldn't be loved or accepted
because of what they considered flaws.
You're not broken, you're beautiful.
You're perfect.
You're everything.*

PROLOGUE

Aiden

"I WILL TAKE HIM," I TOLD LANE, THE MC PRESIDENT.

Wilder set my son in my arms. In that moment my entire life changed. Everything stopped and it was just me and this baby.

I am a member of the Grim Sinners MC. We were taking down a human trafficking ring when we found this baby, around four months old, alone in the basement.

We weren't sure who would take him, and none of us wanted him to go into foster care.

So I stepped up. I decided to take him and raise him as my own. It may have been stupid, but it's something I will never regret.

One of the things I've always wanted is to be a dad, I thought.

Why not start now? This baby needs a home, someone to love him, and I can do that.

I know it won't be easy, but he deserves it.

We both need each other.

1

GRACE

"GET OFF OF THE ROAD!" I SCREAM, STICKING MY HEAD OUT THE window. My road rage is getting the better of me.

This guy is barely moving in the fast lane and, on top of that, I am late for my softball game. I got caught up volunteering at the community center and lost all track of time.

I am the coach for a Little League softball team. What does it say when a coach is late for her own game? I stop at the red light, banging my head on the steering wheel.

The driver swerves into my lane, trying to hit me. I gasp and clutch my steering wheel, swerving into the next lane, almost hitting a truck. The driver of the truck slams his brakes, rolling down his window. I grimace waiting for the chewing-out I'm about to get.

He's definitely not what I expected. First off: can I say *beautiful*? He is wearing glasses that give him this sexy Superman vibe, but Superman wouldn't be covered in tattoos.

Oh no, this man is pure sin.

Without thinking I yell out, "Sorry about that, hot stuff!" I feel my face get hot, and I roll up my window and floor it.

I can't believe I just did that! I have never done anything like that. I rub my warm cheek and turn on some music as a distraction from what a fool I just made of myself.

A minute later the softball field comes into view, and I let out a deep breath. Right on time.

Some of the parents are already here, and Tiffany, the star of the team, is already on the field practicing pitching. She is always the first one on the field and the last one off. She is absolutely amazing, and I see her playing in college one day if she continues at this pace.

"Hi Grace, do you need help?" Amelia asks, and I smile at her. She's Tiffany's mom, and she's an amazing helper. She is always ready to do a bake sale or help me chaperone away games, and she's very supportive of all the girls. Hell, all the team parents have been amazing. They've made donations and bought new equipment, and they are always at all the games, even the ones hours away.

"You can help me carry the snacks for the girls." I open the back of my SUV, which is piled high with a million different things.

I am a softball coach, and I volunteer at the local community center for kids. I fill my days with helping others.

My day job is...well...I am a trust fund kid. My grandparents left me everything. That left me with more than enough money to live on very comfortably for...well...forever.

At the local community center, I work with kids who have been abused or are in difficult family situations. We are their escape, and we provide meals.

Doing what I do is hard. It is so hard to see kids suffering when there's nothing I can do about it. All I can do is try to make their day better while they are there.

"I heard this team was pretty tough," Amelia says, looking at the field where the other team is practicing.

I nod. "They might be good, but we are better—and we have

heart." I wink at Tiffany, who is helping another girl practice her batting. Tiffany beams and pulls her mask over her face. She throws a perfect pitch to the girl, and the ball sails across the field.

"That's my girls!" I yell.

Some of the MC guys pop out of nowhere and help us unload everything. I thank them and go out onto the field with the girls, and I pull my hair back into a ponytail. "Tiffany! Cindy!" I have them go with me to talk to the umpires and the coaches of the opposite team.

Yeah, it's just me, myself, and I. I'm the only coach, and I kind of prefer it this way—I don't have anyone else to answer to.

The two guys who coach the other team are older than me by at least twenty years. They look at each other and smirk. I try to resist the urge to roll my eyes. They have underestimated me.

We shake hands. "Where's your head coach?" one of them asks.

I giggle, putting on my best, most friendly smile. "I am the head coach." I go back to ignoring them and listen to the umpire talk about the rules.

They walk off. "Good luck. You guys are going to need it."

I narrow my eyes, and Tiffany huffs beside me. "I think someone's wanting their butt kicked," Tiffany says way too loudly, and I suck in my bottom lip trying to control my laughter. They are kind of asking for it.

"Let's show them." I wink and we walk across the field to the other girls. Tiffany immediately fills them in on what's going on. I sit back and let it happen—you know why? That will put a fire under their butts, making them more determined to win.

I gather up the girls, and I bend down closer to their level. "Alright girls, they may have a fancier school, but we have heart and we have each other's backs. Let's show them not to underestimate us."

"Let's go!" they all scream at once and run across the field.

The other team is batting first, and I watch proudly as my girls run to their positions.

I lean against the wall of the dugout. One of the girls on the opposite team is up to bat, and I gnaw on my bottom lip. With a nod, Tiffany throws the ball.

"Strike!" The umpire yells and I grin.

"That's my girl!" I yell. Amelia is jumping up and down in the stands.

"Hey, hot stuff," someone says directly behind me. I jump and gape at the sight of the man I called "hot stuff" earlier, when I had the road rage incident.

"I...uh." I stop, not knowing what to say, and he just continues to grin at me. Then I look down at the vest he is wearing. Grim Sinners MC.

My mouth dries as I connect the dots, and I close my eyes and turn around. Maybe he will just leave?

"The view isn't bad back here either, darlin'," he teases.

I cover my face and walk away, closer to the girls. I can hear him chuckling, and my embarrassment grows.

Can the ground just swallow me up right now?

"Strike!"

I grin and clap. Tiffany has that shit-eating grin on her face; she knows she is good.

Amelia's husband, Lane, is already out of his seat, standing at the fence. "That's my baby!" he yells and I laugh. Give it ten minutes and he will be standing right next to me, with half of the MC. They get torn into pieces at these games, especially the ones where it's a close call.

Did I mention that we are undefeated? I am proud of that fact. We have practiced and practiced, before and after school. We want to hit the nationals, and we are determined to win.

"Strike!" One out and two more to go.

The other two strike out without hitting even one ball. They switch out, and all my girls run back to the dugout.

The other coach glares at me from across the field, and I high five everyone on the team. "I am so proud of you girls!"

Amelia is handing out drinks. Like I said, she is amazing.

"Thank you, Amelia."

She waves me off.

Tiffany is batting first; she is just as good with a bat as she is at pitching. She is a weapon all around. I walk with Tiffany to the batter's box, and she bounces slightly on her feet, twirling her bat. She sets her stance and steadies herself.

I feel someone standing beside me, and I see it's Lane. I told you it wouldn't take long.

I wish all fathers were like him. He's a huge source of support to Tiffany, and Amelia is just out-of-this-world amazing.

The pitcher throws the ball, but it's too far to the left.

"Ball!" the umpire yells.

The pitcher throws again, and I know Tiffany is going to hit it.

Crack! The ball sails toward the back of the field, she runs, and the girls scream. She gets to second base before the other team catches up to her.

"That's my girl!" Lane yells, and I laugh as Tiffany gives him a thumbs-up.

This continues for a long time. We have almost twenty runs in before they finally get us out.

Tiffany prepares herself to pitch, and I wince at the ass-chewing the girls on the other team are getting from their coaches.

"Fucking douchebag." I start at the sound of the voice beside me. It's the hot guy from earlier.

I play it cool. "Yeah, they kind of are." I finally decide to put my big-girl panties on. "I am Grace."

He looks me up and down, grinning. "Yes you are."

I roll my eyes and laugh. "Thank you, I guess."

He laughs with me and pushes his glasses further up his nose.

He is rocking the bad-boy nerd look very well. "I am Aiden. It's nice to officially meet you."

"It's nice to meet you too." I smile and turn back to the game; then he leaves and I think that is it.

He comes back holding a baby, who is probably around six months old.

"He's so cute," I coo, and my hands are itching to hold him.

"Thank you." Aiden kisses the top of his head, and my ovaries are gone in that second. Hello! A hot guy holding a baby?

Tiffany does her single nod and throws.

"Strike!"

I look sideways at Lane and Amelia. We love to see them win, but we don't want someone to be completely butchered.

One of the girls hits the ball, and I know Tiffany slowed down the pitch for her, but one of our girls catches it in the air.

Out.

After they are out, the coaches yell for a meeting. I am waved over. I run over, and the nicer of the two tells me that they forfeit.

I reach out. "Good game." I smile. The nicer one shakes my hand, and the other turns tail and walks away.

"Well, okay," I murmur to myself.

I wave the girls over, and they shake hands with the other team, telling each other, "Good game."

"I am so proud of you girls tonight! No practice tomorrow, rest up for our next game." I smile and they all gather their stuff.

"So, hot stuff, can I get your number?"

I smile and turn around. Aiden is standing behind me, still carrying that precious baby.

"Maybe, but where is his mom?" I want to get that straight out there. I am sure I could have asked another way, but I don't beat around the bush anymore.

"He doesn't have one."

My heart sinks. How awful is that? "I am sorry," I whisper,

feeling like a total bitch for the way I asked that question. I just assumed they had broken up.

He shakes his head. "No, don't be sorry for that." He steps closer, and I have to stop the urge to step back. "So can I?" he asks again, that smirk returning to his face.

What should I do? Should I say yes? Am I just wasting my time? Relationships and me just don't work for some reason.

Well, we both know the reasons, Grace.

Fuck it. "Sure."

For the first time, I see him smile—it's deadly.

He hands me his phone, and I put my number in and call myself so I'll have his number too. "I'll be in touch, hot stuff." He winks and walks away.

Did that really just happen?

Is this a movie? I almost took out a guy in a road rage incident, and now I'm going on a date with that very same guy.

I smile and get busy putting the rest of my stuff away. "Bye, girls!" I yell as they leave with their parents. I grab my bag and walk to my SUV.

I climb into my vehicle and wait until every last person has left before I leave. I have to get to the center so I can finish preparing snacks for the kids to take home.

When I walk into the center, I am greeted by blinding smiles. "Gracie!" a few of them yell and run toward me.

I laugh and bend down so I can hug them.

"I was waiting for you, Miss Gracie," Leah, one of the regulars here, tells me. She is precious. She has long blonde hair, in pigtails, and she's wearing a sweater with a pair of jeans. Her clothes are a little the worse for wear. She is around seven years old.

"I'm sorry I'm a little late, honey. Want to help me prepare the lunch bags?"

She nods frantically and holds my hand.

We walk together to the kitchen. "Do you want to grab the bags out of the drawer?"

She lets go of my hand and does as she was asked.

I push the container of snacks and drinks into the middle of the floor. I sit down on the floor, and she joins me.

"Want me to open the bags for you, Miss Gracie?" She moves from her knees onto her bottom. That's when I notice bruising on her shins. The sad thing is most of the kids here have been through something like this at some point in their lives. This is their safe haven. This is the place where they can be kids and leave everything at the door.

I put sandwiches, fruit, water, and other things into the bags. It gives me major peace of mind knowing the children will have food tonight. I love all the kids here. I wish I could just adopt every single one of them and give them the lives they deserve.

"Miss Gracie, I wish I could be a part of your softball team."

I put down the bag I was holding. "If you had permission from your parents, I would love to have you."

She grips the bottom of her shirt, and her eyes light up. "Really, Miss Gracie?"

I laugh at how excited she is. "Yes, really!"

She grins and goes back to helping me. We work in sync and get everything done in record time. We put everything in the container, carry it to the front room, and put it by the door so they can grab their snacks as they leave.

Leah is bouncing around the room talking to every kid, helping them with their crafts, and I just sit back watching her.

"Hey, Gracie."

I look over at Marie, my best friend and another volunteer. She is here every evening, tutoring the ones who need it. She is a schoolteacher.

"Hey Marie, how was school today?"

She wipes her forehead with the back of her hand. "Exhausting."

I look at her, concerned; she really looks worn down.

"Why don't you leave early. I am sure that I can handle everything myself today."

She puts down the washcloth she was holding. "Are you sure? I am pretty beat."

I wave my arm. "It's nothing. Go rest."

She smiles at me. "Thank you so much, Grace. You're the best." She gives me a side hug, and I pat her back.

I finish cleaning everything up and preparing for tomorrow evening, when we will reopen. I take out a piece of paper and write my name and number on it for Leah. "Leah, honey, can you come here for a second?"

She runs over, and I sit down on one of the lunch-table benches. I hand her the piece of paper. "This is my number. Call me anytime, even if it's just to talk, and especially if you need anything."

She looks at the piece of paper for a few seconds before she takes it. "Thank you, Miss Gracie." She gives me a quick hug.

"Everyone ready?" Henry, our bus driver, will be taking everyone home. He is a bus driver for the school system, but he volunteers for this every evening.

All the kids run to the front of the building, grabbing their bags of snacks on the way out. The last one is Leah, and she looks back at me one last time before she steps out.

My heart immediately hurts. I can't stand the thought of them being hurt or scared once they get home.

This is such a hard thing to do. It's difficult seeing so many of these kids go through things and there's nothing I can do.

Some of them are in foster care. Some of them are in bad home situations, and the system often does nothing.

I saw the bruise on Leah, and I know that will haunt me. I need to check in with the director of the center before I can report the abuse. I close my eyes and let out a deep breath, trying to calm myself.

I'm ready to crawl into bed with a glass of wine and just let the day disappear.

HANDS, touches, pain.

I wake up, sitting up in bed, my heart pounding. I clench my eyes shut, trying to ignore everything that just happened in my brain.

A few minutes pass before I allow myself to sink back into bed. I pull the blankets up around me. On either side of me is a huge body pillow. They make me feel safe and stop the feeling something is going to drag me out of bed.

At moments like this, I wish I had someone to come home to. Someone to hold. Most of all, someone to love me.

Me and relationships literally don't work. I think I have a douchebag magnet pressed onto my forehead, because that is literally all I attract. But I always shut down the budding relationship before it gets anywhere.

One thing I know is that I don't want to get hurt, and if I can protect myself, why not?

It's a lonely life though. I dedicate myself to helping others, and I know that I have been neglecting myself. But when I do try, it just ends badly. I don't know what it would be like if a man treated me well, which is why I have pushed dating to the back of my mind.

Taking my phone off the nightstand, I notice that I have a text. I open it.

Hey, it's Aiden. Do you want to grab dinner tomorrow?

Oh wow, I never thought that he would actually message me. I sit up before I reply.

Wait, should I do this? Is this a good idea?

What do I have to lose? I am already in a lonely existence.

Hey, that sounds great. Seven?

I put my phone back on the nightstand and try to go back to sleep, this time with a smile on my face and without the nightmares that I try to forget.

2

GRACE

AROUND FOUR O'CLOCK THE BUS DROPS THE KIDS OFF IN FRONT OF the center, and I open the door.

I have been here since around two o'clock so I could prepare their dinner. We don't have nearly enough volunteers, so I am a jack-of-all-trades. I even took one of the kids to the doctor one time; her parents had asked me to because they had to work.

My goal is just to make a difference in one of these babies' lives. I want this to be a place where they can escape.

"Miss Gracie?" I look around and see Leah in the doorway. She's wearing the same clothes as yesterday.

"Hey sweetheart, how are you today?" I set a container of juice on the counter.

She slips into the room. "I talked to my father, and he said that I can play softball." She grins ear to ear.

"How exciting! I will give you the paperwork before you leave, so he can sign." I touch the top of her head. "Do you want to help me?"

She takes the carton of juice and leans back at the weight. "You sure you have it?" I reach out to catch it if necessary

She nods. "I got it, Miss Gracie."

I grin at her retreating form; she is absolutely precious. I take the fries out of the stove. We let them vote on what they wanted to eat, and we're having burgers and fries. I put the fries on their plates, which are sitting on a cart, and push the cart into the cafeteria.

"Hi, Miss Gracie!" a few of the kids yell, and Leah sits down at the end of the table. I put a plate in front of her.

"Thank you."

One by one, I pass their plates out; then I grab my own and sit down with them. This is my favorite part of the day with them; I can get down on their level.

"Miss Gracie, I scored a ninety-five percent on my spelling test," Matthew, one of the older kids, tells me.

"Wow, congrats. I knew you could do it," I say. We actually studied together last week.

One by one, I have a conversation with each of them, and once they are finished they set their plates on the cart. Someone will wash them later. I need to get ready for my date. "Everyone get started on your homework." They all run to get their backpacks. "I will be back in a few minutes to check on you guys."

I already have my bag in the bathroom, and I hurry in to change. I put on a pair of white skinny jeans and a royal-blue open-shouldered shirt. I take out my curling wand, and I'm curling my hair when I hear a knock on the door. I peer out and see Leah.

"Can I watch?"

I smile. "Sure, honey." I push the door open, and she steps inside and sits down on the toilet.

I style my hair in loose, wavy curls that frame my face. My hair is long and dark brown with blond highlights. I have big brown eyes and a few freckles covering my cheeks and nose. My nose is small and pert, and my lips are large. I have a dimple on each cheek and high cheekbones.

My body is curvy; I have a big butt, big boobs, and a small

waist. I love my body; it's something that I've always liked about myself.

"You're very pretty, Miss Gracie," Leah tells me.

"Thank you, sweetheart. So are you."

She beams at me happily. "You really think so?"

"Yes, you're very beautiful, but you're also beautiful in here." I point to her chest.

She walks over and hugs me, her face pressed into my stomach. "Thank you, Miss Gracie."

I hug her back. "You're welcome, sweetheart."

She lets me go and I finish my hair. The closer it gets to time for Aiden to pick me up, here at the center, the more nervous I am. I'm scared for so many reasons. Most of my dates haven't been the best; it seems that I attract the crazy ones. I'm also nervous because Aiden is, hands down, the most attractive guy I have gone out with. I just hope that it goes well tonight.

I finish my hair and touch up my makeup; then I am done. I stand back from the mirror, checking one last time.

I am as ready as I ever will be.

IT'S ALMOST SEVEN O'CLOCK, and all the kids in the center have gone home. I made sure to give Leah my number and the papers to sign to play softball.

My phone buzzes in my back pocket, and I see a text from Aiden, letting me know he is outside. That's when the nerves hit me full force. First off—holy hell, I am going on a date with the most beautiful man I have ever seen. I close my eyes, trying to stop my growing panic. What if he's too much?

My fear is buried deep. I'm afraid of men in general. I have seen the worst of humanity, and I'm terrified of encountering anything like that again. Because if someone who is supposed to love and care for you more than anything can hurt you, why wouldn't someone else?

Stop! I command myself. I need to stop these thoughts from thundering through my brain or I will be in a funk.

Throwing caution to the wind, I text Aiden and let him know that I am on my way out. I step outside and lock the door behind me. He's standing outside of his truck, grinning at me.

I swallow hard. His arms are folded across his chest; they're covered in tattoos and his muscles are bulging. He has on his glasses. They give him that sexy geek look but I know, underneath all of that, he is pure badass.

One, two, three, I chant to myself, and I start in his direction.

"Wow, you look absolutely amazing!"

I smile widely. "Thank you, Aiden." I can feel my cheeks start to warm under his gaze.

He splits the distance between us and walks with me to the passenger side of his truck. He opens the door for me.

"Thank you."

I climb inside and he shuts the door. I close my eyes, begging myself to stay calm and not overthink every single thing. That is one of the biggest things I wish I didn't do. I see things and I think the worst. It's especially bad in relationships; when someone comes on too strong, it literally ruins the whole relationship. I get scared and crawl within myself, and I just have to get out of there.

Aiden gets in and starts the truck, and we're off. I place my hands in my lap, rubbing my thumbs together. It's a nervous habit.

He breaks the silence. "Are you from here originally?"

"Yes, I have lived here my whole life." I take a second to look at him while he's driving. He really is beautiful.

"Did you go to school here too?"

"Yeah, I went to Fairmont High School."

He slows down the truck and looks at me; then he grins widely. "How old are you?"

"Twenty-five."

He throws his head back, laughing loudly. My eyes widen at the sight of him letting go so easily. "I dated you when I was fifteen."

Wait, what? I think back to my first boyfriend. We dated for a few months before going our separate ways. He was my first kiss.

My mouth pops open as the dots connect. The glasses, the dark hair and eyes. "Oh my god! Aidey?" I used to call him that.

He nods, still smiling. "It's my Gracie."

I fall back against my seat laughing. Who would have thought this would happen? I know one thing: I immediately feel better because I know him. "Wow, I never expected to see you again. Let alone go out on a date with you," I confess as everything slowly starts to sink in.

"Gracie, it seems that fate had a play in this." He winks, and I laugh again because he is still a big cheese ball like he was back then.

"Do you remember what you got me for my birthday?" I ask him. I still have it, actually.

He blinks a few times before he chuckles. "I gave you a box that had my picture glued to the bottom of it. I said I was the best gift you could have, and then we started dating immediately after that."

I snort. I was so impressed with how cocky he was that I agreed to be his girlfriend. Plus, I always copied his homework, so it was a win-win. It's hard to believe that was so long ago.

He looks at me, flashing that shit-eating grin. "Damn, I was good."

I laugh. "I guess you were. I was impressed." It's hard to believe that I am going on a date with my first-ever boyfriend and I didn't even realize it until he mentioned it.

His looks have completely changed. Back when I dated him— and mind you we were both fourteen at the time—he was a major dork.

I would not call him that now. He does have that slight vibe, but he has this bad-boy vibe that every single girl secretly loves.

A few minutes later we pull up outside the best restaurant in town; sometimes it takes weeks to get a reservation. "How did you get in?" I ask him.

"We own it." He gets out before I can start throwing a million different questions at him. I have heard the MC has a lot of businesses, but I never expected this place to be one of them.

I open my door, and he holds out his hand for me to take. I set my palm on his. After he helps me out of the truck, he doesn't let go of my hand like I thought he would. We walk hand and hand to the front door. Don't ask me why this is such a big deal to me, but as someone who has always had issues with being touched, every little thing is a big deal.

He holds the door open for me, and we walk inside. The hostess is standing holding two menus. I peek over at Aiden just as he smiles at me. His smile reaches all the way to his eyes, making him ten times more beautiful. It lights his whole face. When I was fourteen he constantly had me laughing; he was always doing sweet and cheesy things.

A hand is pressed to the small of my back, and I look over at Aiden as we follow the waitress to our table, next to a window overlooking the town. Aiden pulls out my chair for me, and I sit down with a smile. Such a gentleman. Then he sits down in front of me. My nerves were extremely bad in the beginning, but I'm relieved that I kind of know him, even though we were very young.

"Wow, it's really hard to believe that it's you, Aiden." I study his face. He still has the glasses, but everything else has completely changed. His hairstyle, the tattoos—and he is huge. He is probably around six-three or -four.

"And you are very different, CiCi." The corner of his mouth slightly curls.

I grin. For some unknown reason, he called me CiCi from the very beginning. "I haven't heard that name in such a long time."

He leans forward on his elbows. "Of course you haven't. I was the only one who called you that."

Butterflies swarm my belly. "You were." I look down at my menu. I can feel him looking at me, but I don't dare look up. The longer I ignore his stares, the hotter my face becomes.

"You were beautiful back then, but now you're absolutely stunning, CiCi."

My mouth opens slightly at his confession. I put my menu down and smile widely. "Thank you, Aiden. You're still as big of a sweetheart as you were back then."

He sits back in his seat hard, glaring at me slightly, but I can see the laughter in his eyes. "Now, a man like me isn't sweet, CiCi."

I laugh because the only thing that can describe this man is sweet. I wink at him. "Your secret is safe with me, Aiden."

He chuckles, running his hand across the top of his head, slightly mussing up his hair.

"Hi, what can I get you guys to drink?" the waitress asks.

"I will take a glass of red wine," I tell her and Aiden orders a beer, which is one thing that I can't stomach.

"I saw you as a red wine girl. Still reading those romance novels?" He winks.

My stomach flips. "I can't believe that you remembered that."

He throws his head back laughing, a vein popping out on the side of his neck. Once he gains control of himself, he grins at me. "How can I forget?" My face burns with embarrassment.

This was the first time that Aiden ever came to my house. I was scared out of my mind, but I was so excited

We snuck off to my room. We sat around and binge-watched movies for a couple of hours, made out, and just cuddled, but then I went to the bathroom.

I came back, and he had found my stash of romance novels. I

know, at fourteen, that is not something I should have been reading, but I devoured them.

I remember standing there, horrified. I had left my bookmark on a sex scene. Aiden looked up at me with a shit-eating grin on his face.

What did I do, you may ask? I ran outside and hid.

"Imagine my shock, looking over at the table and seeing a full-blown romance novel," he says. "Then you ran outside and hid from me for thirty minutes." He bursts out laughing again.

I lean back in my chair with my arms crossed, pouting because he is calling me out. He stops laughing, eyeing me. "You know I'm teasing you, CiCi."

I stop my fake pouting before I start laughing. "I was mortified, especially at fourteen and being caught red-handed." I unfold my silverware from my napkin.

"Yeah, especially considering what I read."

I gasp dramatically and throw my napkin across the table, hitting him in the chest.

"Ouch, killer," he says.

The waiter breaks the moment as she brings our drinks. "Do you guys need a few more minutes to order?"

"Yes please." I haven't even looked at the menu. I take a sip of my wine.

"I figured you would order the crab legs, since that is your favorite—or it used to be."

My eyes widen. "You remember that?"

He shrugs. "I remember a lot about you, CiCi."

I smile. How absolutely out-of-this-world sweet is he? I gaze at him.

He glances at his menu for a second before looking at me again. "What is it?" he asks.

"I remember a lot about you too." I wink at him, and I have to say I am mighty proud of myself for accomplishing that feat. It's taken many years to learn to wink without closing both eyes at the same time.

He lays his menu down on the table. "Oh yeah, tell me some things."

I smirk. "I remember, first off, that you're a major momma's boy."

He laughs. "She spoiled you too, CiCi." He is one hundred percent correct. I really did love his mother. Honestly, she was someone I needed very much in my life. Yes, I was fourteen but I was dealing with A LOT.

I lived with my grandparents at the time. My grandpa was really amazing, but my grandmother seemed to not like me very much. It was as if I were the reason for all of her troubles, even if she stubbed her toe. I'm not even going to get started on my parents.

"She really did. How is she doing, by the way?" I ask.

"She is doing great, enjoying babysitting tonight." I grin at that. She was probably chomping at the bit to babysit.

I know one thing: I am very curious about where his baby's mom is. I know that she isn't around, but I don't know how to approach the topic. I open my mouth to ask, but then I close it. What if that is in bad taste?

He is studying me. "You want to know about Reid's mom, right?"

I wince on the inside, being called out. "You don't have to tell me, Aiden," I whisper.

"He is adopted. I adopted him a couple of months ago from a trafficking ring."

I stare at him in complete shock. I never expected that. I honestly thought that Reid's mother just left Aiden to take care of the baby by himself.

"Wow, Aiden, I had no clue." I don't know what to say, but that is an amazing thing he is doing.

"He may not be mine biologically, but he is my son."

In that moment the way I see Aiden completely changes; my respect for him increases tenfold. "You're pretty amazing, you know that?" I had to say something because not many people would do what he is doing without a second thought.

"CiCi, it's no hardship for me—this is my baby. That is all there is to it." He brushed off the compliment like it was nothing, but I know one thing: I am not brushing it off that easily.

"If you say so."

WE STEP out of the restaurant around a hour later, and the cool night is refreshing. Aiden is walking close to my side. I have noticed that he is always watching his surroundings.

"Do you want to go night fishing?" he asks.

I gasp dramatically, holding my chest. "Do I ever? I am down to go fishing all the time."

He laughs at me. "I have a lake right by my house. Want to head there? You can borrow one of my fishing poles."

I take his hand and practically pull him to the truck. "Come on, I can hear the fish calling my name."

He laughs and opens the truck door for me, and he helps me inside. He is about to be shown how to fish.

WE PULL up outside a large black iron gate. He reaches out and presses some buttons on the pad, and it swings open.

I sit up further in my seat. We start up a long driveway, and on the other side of the road, a black fence leads all the way to the end of the property, where his house is.

He lives in a large log cabin with huge windows in the front. The inside of the house gives off a luminous golden glow.

"Oh wow, your house is beautiful, Aiden."

He looks at me; I can see his eyes in the glow of the lights on his dashboard. He pulls up in front of the cabin, and I open my door and step out.

I am really proud of him. I am really proud of the way he has turned out. It's amazing to think that I knew fourteen-year-old Aiden, the nerd who people made fun of but who was just the sweetest.

"Do you want me to get you a jacket or anything?" he asks as I follow him toward his garage, which is opening.

"I think I will be fine, but I can take one anyway?"

As we get closer to the garage, I see a whole wall covered with fishing poles, and under it is every kind of essential you could want or need.

I grin. "I do believe you're my kind of man." I walk straight to a fishing pole just like mine and take it from the wall. I turn around, smirking. "Are you prepared to be outfished?" I tease him.

He gets a wicked gleam in his eye. "Oh honey, I'd like to see you try." He takes a couple of jackets from a shelf. Then he walks over to a mini-fridge and takes out some live bait. He is one hundred percent my kind of guy.

"Hand me your pole and I will tie it down until we get to the lake."

I hand him the pole and look at the side-by-side. "Do you want me to get in?" He gives me a slight nod, and I get in on the passenger's side.

His arms flex as he ties down the poles, and I take the time to admire the way his muscles move and his messy hair frames his face. He has grown into a fine-looking man, that is for sure. He finishes tying down the pole and gets in the side-by-side. He starts it up, and I close my eyes as a sudden surge of fear hits me.

All alone in a dark place, and no one can help you. You are completely alone. Your phone is in the truck.

I bite my lip and try to stop the erratic thoughts in my head. I don't want to have these thoughts, and I know that he would not hurt me. This fear arises over the smallest things.

I open my eyes as Aiden backs out of the garage. "Here, Cici." He puts the jacket in my lap so I can cover myself if needed.

"Thank you." I feel much better. These things just hit me out of nowhere. I hate to say it, but that is a huge factor in why my relationships have not worked. I never let them reach their full potential. I just run, and I don't want to do that anymore.

I snap myself out of my thoughts before I can dive too deeply into them. I sit up and plaster on a smile, pretending that I am not fighting an internal war.

3

He pulls to a stop in front of a dock, and I open the small door to the side-by-side as he unties the poles. I look up into the night sky, loving seeing all the stars and being away from everything. I just breathe, relax, and let go.

"Ready?" he asks and I nod. I follow him down the short path to the boat dock.

"It's really beautiful here," I tell him. The water and the calmness are intoxicating. I sit down on the edge of the dock and take off my shoes so my toes can be in the water.

He sits beside me, and I'm hyperaware of our legs touching slightly.

He hands me some bait, and I bait my hook and throw my line out into the water. "This is kind of crazy, isn't it? I was thinking I was going out on a date with someone completely new, but then it was you. It's kind of wild."

He grins. "Yeah, I was thinking that I'd just met this hot softball coach, and now it's CiCi. I am thrilled though. I have thought about you quite a bit over the years."

Happiness flows through me and I smile. "I have thought about you too. I always wondered what happened to you."

I look over at him, trying to wrap my head around all of this. I feel my pole jerk, and I jump up and start to reel in my line. "Yes!" I say loudly, and I back up so I don't fall in. I pull the fish out of the water; it's a big bass.

"Damn." He takes out his phone, and I smile as he takes the picture.

"Now try to beat that." I put the fish back into the water.

"Oh, it's on."

I laugh under my breath and sit beside him, itching to get another bite so I can out-fish him.

"How are your grandparents?" he asks.

Ouch, that's a sore subject. "They both passed away."

We sit in silence for a minute. I can feel him looking at me, but I don't want to see his look of pity so I keep my gaze focused on the water. He knows that they were the only family I had left. They were it. My grandma wasn't the best to me, of course, but it was better than nothing, right? My grandpa, on the other hand? I was really close to him.

"I am really sorry for your loss, CiCi," he says softly, touching the small of my back.

I finally bring myself to look at him. "That was years ago. It was a few months after I turned twenty-one." My grandma died first, then my grandpa. I was alone but I finally had time to heal.

He touches my hand, getting my attention. "I can still feel bad that it happened to you, Gracie."

On the inside I am freaking out because that was so unbelievably sweet. "That was so sweet," I tell him.

His face falls and I laugh. "I am sorry if that ruins your badass image."

He laughs and scoots a little closer to me, but this time I move closer to him. He is radiating heat and it's kind of chilly.

He gets a bite and reels in his line, and I fall to the side laughing at the sight of his little bluegill.

"Ha ha ha." He fake laughs, and I wipe the tears from my eyes. That was absolutely hilarious.

I am still lying on my back and, from the corner of my eye, I see him put his pole down so he can lie down beside me.

We lie side by side, the stars above us. He intertwines our fingers, and I smile and look over at him.

I don't care what he pretends to be; he will always be a softy to me.

Aiden

It fucking hit me like a ton of bricks that it was Gracelyn. We dated when I was fifteen years old and went our separate ways. But she was my first love and my first girlfriend, and I've always thought about her throughout the years.

It's fucking wild that I never realized it until we went out tonight. It's like fate had a play in all of this.

I watch her stare up into the sky. I know one fucking thing: she is not going to just slide out of my life again.

I want to know her, the woman. I want to know what she has been up to the last ten years.

She yawns loudly.

"Tired?" I ask.

She nods. "It's been a long day."

"Come on. I will take you home." I sit up and take her hand, helping her up off the dock.

Gracie

When we pull up in front of the center, where I left my car, nervousness hits me. I have many, many flashbacks of moments when the date was over and the man thought he needed to be rewarded for buying me dinner. This sets off a chain reaction in my brain, telling me I need to get out of there.

I unlock my car door, and he opens it for me.

"Thank you, I have had a lot of fun."

"Me too, Gracie. Want to grab lunch tomorrow?"

I find myself nodding instantly. "I would love that." I really would.

He leans forward, his hand touching my cheek gently and, much to my utter shock, his lips touch my forehead softly. I close my eyes, just basking in the feel of his lips on me. Lips that aren't asking more of me. Lips that don't want to force me to do things before I am ready. This is pure, unadulterated respect, and my respect for him grows tenfold.

"Be safe, text me when you've made it safely."

I nod. "You be safe too."

I get in my car and he shuts my door. As I pull out of the parking lot, I look in the rearview mirror and see him watching me leave.

"Holy shit," I whisper to myself. I just can't believe all of that happened. I went into the date thinking one thing and came out thinking something completely different.

I wonder what tomorrow will bring?

4

GRACE

I look at the clock on the wall and it's noon. Aiden will be here any minute, and I have to say I am pretty excited.

I woke up this morning, and the first thing I did was check my phone to see if I had any messages from Aiden. I did. He wished me good morning, and I have to admit I was way too excited over one little text.

So I got dressed in a pair of jeans and a loose black V-neck, which is comfortable but very flattering. I went to the center to make sure everything was up and running for dinner and game night. Every Friday night we have a game night, and all the kids can stay until nine o'clock. We have movies, fun games, and snacks, and once a month we all stay for a lock-in. It gives them something to look forward to, because many of them don't have that.

At the door we have a wish box, where the kids can put in notes about what they need or want. One way or another, we try to make sure that happens. Usually it comes out of my own pocket. I have been blessed with a lot; why not share that?

I hear a motorcycle outside. Do you think? I start toward the door and look out to see Aiden sitting, right out front, on his bike.

Oh yeah, I am hopping on the back of that.

I feel nervous but very excited at the same time. Last night was an amazing date, and I want to see what will happen next. I push open the door and step outside.

He smiles at me. "You ready?"

Am I? I am ready as I am going to be. He reaches into his saddlebag and takes out a leather jacket. "Put this on, sweetheart, and this." He takes out a helmet.

I slip on both of them, and I take his outstretched hand and swing my leg over the seat behind him. Okay, that was easier than I thought it would be. He looks back at me. "Scoot closer to me, babe, and hang on." I scoot closer until my front is flush against his back and my arms are around his waist.

He starts the bike; then we are off. My stomach sinks from the feeling of riding the bike for the first time. It's nerve-racking but I can see why it's intoxicating; it's very freeing. I close my eyes and enjoy being in the moment. This is something I need to do more often; I have to fight the habit of overthinking everything.

When we stop at a red light, I open my eyes. Aiden's muscles are bulging as he squeezes the handlebars. His thighs are thick in his jeans as he braces us. It should be a crime for a man to look like this.

Someone pulls up beside us; a woman is staring at him through the window. Bless your heart, girl. I know exactly how you feel.

The light turns green, and we pull into the parking lot of a pretty nice restaurant.

Inside we are seated instantly. I'm sure I have major helmet hair and look less than amazing, but I can't find it in myself to really care.

Aiden doesn't sit across from me like I thought he would, but right next to me, and my body is instantly alert to his every movement.

"How does it feel knowing you got beat last night?" I tease

him. I continue to look at my menu, but you couldn't take the grin off my face if you tried.

He laughs. "I have no clue what you're talking about."

"Mhm. How is Reid today?"

Aiden's face completely transforms at the mention of his son. How beautiful is that? "He is amazing today. Bailey is watching him for me." Aiden takes out his phone and shows me his screensaver, which is a picture of his son.

"He's precious, Aiden. You know, he looks so much like you that you can't tell he's adopted." Reid really does look like a carbon copy of him.

Aiden smiles wider. "He was meant to be mine, it's fate."

I sigh on the inside. "I think that's completely correct, Aiden. You seem to be an amazing dad. He is blessed." Saying that automatically makes me think of myself. I never had a father figure in my life. My grandfather played that role in a way, but it's not the same.

"Thank you. I want to be the best I can be. He deserves it."

Be still my freaking heart. I just stare at him, enraptured, because what man says the things he's saying? Surely not one I've ever met before. I touch his arm without thinking. "You really are the sweetest." I have to repeat myself, because it's one hundred percent true.

He gives me a grin that makes me feel like there's more to Aiden than I think.

Aiden
A couple of hours later

I notice someone ducking out the back door, and I sprint around the house, hot on his ass.

He is trying to scale the fence. I take out my knife and stab his right calf. I hear the thump as the knife glides all the way through to the fence. He screams and lets go. When he hits the ground, the knife sinks further into his leg. Stupid fucker.

I walk over to him, stepping on the hand that is trying to take the knife out of his leg.

His eyes shoot to mine. He pales and scrambles up to a sitting position. "I didn't do anything."

"Did I say you did anything?" I ask, but I know very fucking well what he has done and what he hasn't. He is a part of the trafficking ring, one small notch on a long-ass line of sick fucks. He is one of the guys that kidnaps people and then dumps them on a seller.

"Oh yeah? You mean I didn't just watch you almost kidnap a kid?" I was inside a convenience store, picking up some things for Reid, when I noticed he was lurking behind a counter, staring at this eight-year-old boy. The mom turned away, and he tried to make a grab for the boy, but the child started to scream. So the guy left. I followed him and had our guys run his address. He was one of the guys we had been looking for.

Lucky break, huh?

"I wasn't meaning anything! I just wanted to talk!" He begs.

"Fucker, do you think I am just that dumb? I know who you are." I pick him up off the ground and carry him into his house. I toss him into a kitchen chair and tie him to it. "Now, there are two fucking ways we can do this. It can be hard or it can be really fucking hard. You will answer all of my questions."

He shakes his head.

I start laughing, and his eyes fly open to look at me. "I was hoping you would say that." I bend down and grab the knife, and I rip it out of his leg roughly.

He struggles to get out of the ropes.

"The more you struggle, the faster you're going to bleed out." He is going to die one way or another, but first I am going to get every bit of information out of him. If I can help one kid in a horrible situation, it will be worth it. It fucking kills me on the inside knowing that Reid had been sold and we found him in a fucking basement all by himself. They were trying to hide him. That will forever be burned in my memory. Luckily, we got to him before anything could happen to him.

That is what I am more than thankful for.

"Tell me who you are working for."

He shakes his head, which fucking thrills me to no end. I grab the back of his chair and drag him over to the sink. I push him back so his head is in the sink. I spread a washcloth over his face, turn on the water, and grab the sprayer. I spray the water over the washcloth.

He immediately starts flailing around, struggling, and I just wait a minute before I take the washcloth off.

"Change your mind?" I ask.

"No," he manages to choke out, gasping for air.

I put the washcloth back over his face and pour more water over his face. With my free hand I search through the kitchen drawers until I find exactly what I need.

I set down the pliers on the kitchen table right in front of him. I take the washrag off and set him down on the floor. He tilts to the side and falls over. I laugh. "Oops." I pick him up, and his eyes widen the second he sees the pliers.

"What are you going to do with this?" he stutters.

"I am going to start with your fingernails, one by one, and if that doesn't work I will start cutting, bit by bit, until you have no fingers left. Then if that doesn't work, I will start cutting off your skin."

I bend down so we are eye to eye. "I can torture you for weeks and keep you alive. Don't fuck with me. I will make your life a living hell, and you will wish for me to kill you."

He stares at me for a few seconds before he lets his head fall in defeat. I know I have him. None of these fuckers lasts longer than a few minutes.

I take out my phone and text the guys, letting them know where I am.

A few minutes later they walk inside the house, and I fill them in on what happened.

Lane walks to the fucker tied to the chair. "I heard that you have some information for me?"

The guy, like a fucking faucet, spouts everything we needed to know and more. He tells us exactly where the main man in the operation is located.

Derek steps forward, putting a silencer on his gun. The fucker screams. "I told you everything you wanted to know!"

"Do you honestly think we are just going to let you live, knowing you had a hand in kidnapping kids? That shit is unforgivable." I growl into his face. I take the gun from Derek, press it to the side of the guy's face, and pull the trigger.

I hand the gun back to Derek, who puts it back in his pocket. He just got back from hiding with Brittany. She had someone after her for a long-ass time, but it seems that they found them, so they are back.

One thing is for sure, they came back different and a couple. Wilder is chomping at the bit because that is his sister, but all of us knew it was going to happen.

My phone vibrates in my pocket, and I see it's a text from Gracie.

Gracie: We're having game night tonight at the center, do you want to come?

Me: What time?

Gracie: Six?

Me: Reid and I will be there.

GRACIE

It's six o'clock, and I am extremely nervous because I'm about to officially meet Reid and that is HUGE. I saw him at the game, but this is totally different. I wasn't dating his dad then. Well, technically I had, but you get what I'm saying.

The kids are starting to show up. Leah comes in next, and she runs straight to me holding a piece of paper. "Look, Miss Gracie!" she yells and thrusts the piece of paper in my direction. She has her parent's signature giving her permission to be on my softball team.

"Looks like I have a new member on my team." I wink at her and she beams at me.

"I am just so excited, Miss Gracie! When's practice?" She is practically jumping up and down.

I point across the room. "Sitting on top of my desk is a schedule. Just grab one."

She takes off at a dead sprint, and I laugh at her excitement. I remember being her age—I loved playing. Softball was such a huge part of my life. Everyone needs an escape, and softball was mine. I could have gone really far in the sport, but I preferred to be a coach. I can continue with the sport I love, but I will be the one making a difference in kids' lives.

The door opens and Aiden steps inside, holding Reid and wearing a backpack diaper bag. I am pretty sure that this is the hottest thing on earth. Seeing a hot, beautiful man carrying his child is extremely attractive.

His eyes go directly to me, and I walk over, trying to ignore the nerves in my stomach. "Hi," I say to him before my eyes lock on Reid's. "He's just so precious, Aiden. Can I?" I reach out to hold him.

"Of course." He smiles and gently hands him to me.

It just hits me, hard. The feeling of everything being right. I press my hand to the small of Aiden's back, staring into his face.

Aiden

HOLY FUCKING SHIT. The sight of her holding Reid just changed my entire world.

She is absolutely beautiful, but her holding my son is just perfection. My heart feels like it's going to beat out of my chest.

She finally takes her eyes off of Reid and looks at me. "I think I am going to keep your son."

I laugh. "Why don't I keep both of you?" I say it teasingly but, in the end, I am not really joking. I would love to be around her twenty-four seven.

Reid starts babbling in baby talk and touches the side of her face. Her eyes shoot to mine, and I can see the awe. My boy is already stealing hearts.

"Miss Gracie, I have the paper!" This little girl is probably right around Tiffany's age.

"That's great, sweetheart." Gracie touches the back of her head. The girl is just completely enraptured by her.

Not that I can blame her.

Gracie has this light about her that you just gravitate to. It's still kind of mind-boggling that we have—somehow, in some unknown way—reunited.

I am beyond fucking thrilled.

Gracie

AIDEN, Leah, and I are sitting at the table, with a few other kids, playing UNO. It's turned into a full-out war, and the kids have continually beaten us.

I am still holding Reid. He is asleep, covered with his blanket. He is the best baby—just so happy.

Aiden is sitting next to me, involved with the kids. They are loving having Aiden— especially the boys. They have asked him a million questions about being a biker.

Aiden slams down his card and sits back, grinning. "I won."

They all gasp dramatically. I laugh at their shocked expressions.

"Good job, Aiden," Leah says, being the sweetest little thing, as usual. She stretches her arms above her head, and when her shirtsleeves fall down, I see fingerprint-shaped bruises on her forearm.

I suck in a sharp breath. I dismissed the bruises on her legs, in a way, because I wasn't one hundred percent sure. I look at Aiden to see if he noticed the same thing I did, and he nods. His jaw is tight with anger.

I look at the clock on the wall, and I see it's getting close to time for them to go home. I come up with a plan. "Leah, can you come and help me?"

She jumps up immediately and walks into the kitchen with me.

"Can you sit down here for a minute?" I ask.

She sits down, staring at me, and I can tell she is completely confused. I sit down beside her and try to make myself as small as possible. I don't want to intimidate her. "Sweetheart, can I ask you how you got those bruises on your arms and legs?" I ask her softly.

She pales and I know instantly she is afraid. I wait for her to answer.

"I'm just clumsy, Miss Gracie."

I know she is lying, but I want her to be able to come to me if she is in trouble. "Okay sweetheart, but I want you to have something." I walk over to my purse and take out a prepaid phone; it has my number in it. "I want you to keep this on you, this is our secret. If you ever feel unsafe, call me instantly and I will be there." I give her the phone, and she stares at it for a few beats before looking at me with tears in her eyes.

My heart shatters. This is just hitting way too close to home for me. I was her, I was Leah, and it's breaking me.

"I promise, Miss Gracie."

I lean over and hug her. "I know it's scary—you feel trapped and it's all you have known—but know that there is more to life, okay?"

"Okay," she whispers and hugs me back so tightly, like she doesn't want to let me go.

She finally pulls away and stuffs the phone into her pocket. I run my hand down the back of her head and watch as she walks back into the game room.

I pull out a chair and sit down. I just need to wrap my head around this and figure out what I'm going to do. I can't very well let a child be in an abusive situation and not do anything about it. But it's out of my hands because the director has to be the one to report it, and he is already aware of it.

A hand touches my back. I jump and look over my shoulder at Aiden, who is looking at me, concerned. "Is she okay?" He sits down beside me, holding a sleeping Reid.

"She denied it, but the other day I noticed bruises on her legs. I gave her a phone so she can call me if she's ever in trouble."

He wraps his arm around me, pulling me into his side, comforting me. *He's comforting me.* I close my eyes and just bask in the moment, because this doesn't happen very often.

I am so used to doing every single thing alone—I have always been alone—and this moment means a lot. He cares enough to comfort me when I am upset.

"Thank you." I decide to hug him. I turn around and rest my face on his chest, next to Reid, who is still asleep. I lay my hand on his back, close my eyes, and breathe deeply, letting his scent flow through me. I needed this; this is the first time I have been hugged in such a long time.

A few minutes pass and I pull back, needing to get back to the kids. Aiden continues to look at me intently. "Are you okay?"

I nod immediately. "I'm okay, I just needed the hug," I answer honestly. One thing is for certain: I will always be okay, no matter what happens. I will never give up. I will never give up trying to be happy and be the best I can be.

5

GRACE

The next day

I ARRIVE A FEW MINUTES BEFORE THE GIRLS GET THERE. I HEAR A vehicle and look up to see Aiden pulling in; I am instantly excited. Last night, he kissed me on my forehead once again and waited until I was safely on the road before he left.

I love this. I love that he is giving me the chance to get to know him before he starts to get physical with me.

I have a bit of PTSD. I can't handle sudden aggressive behavior, and I'm a bit anxious when I start dating someone. Aiden is different—I can see that—and this is different. How I feel is different.

He gets out of his truck and opens the back door. Then he takes out a stroller, and I walk over to help him. When he takes out Reid, I walk closer, itching to hold him. "How is my little man today?"

Aiden chuckles and hands me Reid. I sigh with relief at the feeling of rightness. "You didn't miss me?" Aiden teases and I laugh.

I lean my head against his shoulder without thinking. "Of course I did."

Aiden opens the stroller and retrieves the diaper bag. He is just such an amazing father. I know that is what I find most attractive about him. He chose to do this alone. That is something not many people—especially guys—would do. There is so much more to him than meets the eye.

Reid is sucking on his thumb, looking way too adorable in his jeans and T-shirt. "Are you dressed like Daddy today? All you need is a little vest." I run my hand down the back of his head before I buckle him into his stroller. I pull the shade down so the light doesn't bother him. "How is Daddy feeling today?" I ask with a wink.

Aiden rolls his eyes but never takes that smile off his face. "I am much better now, hot stuff."

A few more vehicles pull into the parking lot. Aiden walks with me toward the field, and I notice more than a few softball moms staring at him. I am not jealous; I would be looking too. It just makes me proud that he is here for me.

Tiffany walks over to the dugout carrying her bag. "Hi Tiffany, how are you today?"

She sets her bag down and starts stretching. "I'm good. I heard we have a new girl on the team?"

"Yes. Leah. Do you think...?" I start but Tiffany immediately starts nodding.

"Yes, I will make friends with her."

I laugh because she knows me well.

Lane and Amelia walk over carrying a cooler and snacks. Again, they are a godsend.

"Thank you guys so much!" I walk over to help them.

Amelia waves off my thanks. "This is no big deal. We love to be involved."

I wish all the girls here had parents who are this involved in their kids' lives. Amelia and Lane sit through every practice and game.

The bus pulls in, and the rest of the girls pile into the dugout. Leah is walking by herself without any equipment.

"Oh yeah, I forgot something in my truck," Aiden says and runs across the lot.

Leah walks straight to my side, and I can tell she is nervous.

"I am so glad you're a part of the team."

Her eyes light up. "I am so excited to be here, Miss Gracie."

I am so distracted by Leah and keeping an eye on Reid, I don't notice Aiden until he reaches us. He is holding a softball bag with two bats on the back. The open bag contains all the equipment anyone could need.

I cover my mouth. Is this what I think it is?

"Hey, Leah, I had this stuff just lying around. Do you think you could use it?" Aiden sets the bag down in front of her with a new pair of shoes.

Tears fill my eyes, and her eyes widen as she takes in everything. With a shaking hand, she touches the top of one of the bats.

"Thank you, Aiden, so much," Leah manages to get out through her emotions, and she walks over and hugs him.

I just can't get over how thoughtful this was. He took the time to run to the store today, and he spent a fortune on top-of-the-line equipment.

"How did you know what to get?" I ask him, still in shock.

He nods in the direction of Tiffany, who waves.

"You guys are just amazing people." I tell him. They truly are. People say bikers are just mean and rough people, but they are so much more than that. They have a huge soft side—well, these bikers do.

Without thinking twice, I grab the front of his shirt, pull him down, and stand up on my tiptoes, kissing him hard. He freezes for a second before he presses his hand to the back of my head, taking over the kiss.

I pull back, my hands on his chest. Wow, that was the best kiss I've ever had. It was just a simple kiss, but it was toe-curling.

But the most shocking thing was it was me who kissed him. I have never, ever been that bold until now.

"Absolute perfection," he whispers, touching the side of my face.

We have completely ignored everyone standing around staring at us. It's just me and him in this moment.

"Come on, I will help you with your gear," Tiffany says, completely bringing us out of our moment. I look around and see Amelia trying to hide her grin. Lane is looking everywhere but at us. Aiden smooths my hair over my shoulder, kissing my temple. I smile, butterflies just swarming inside me.

I give Leah a few minutes to get prepared. "Thank you so much for what you have done for her."

"I didn't want her to feel left out. Anything she needs, let me know."

I sigh as my ovaries implode inside my body. Reid babbles in his stroller, and I bend down and shake one of his toys. He reaches forward to take it from me with that beautiful baby grin.

It's six o'clock, and in late March it gets kind of chilly as it turns to evening. Without thinking I take one of the blankets from his diaper bag. It's a thin one, but it will be enough to keep him snug. I take him out of his stroller and wrap him in the blanket.

"Alright you guys, we are running the bases! I will be timing you." They all run out onto the field. I hold Reid throughout practice, as I direct the girls, but what surprises me the most is Leah.

"Leah, are you sure you've never played before?" I ask her, kind of in shock. Tiffany throws the ball to her and, without any direction, Leah hits the ball all the way to the back fence. She runs fast. My girls are good, and one of them retrieves the ball before Leah gets to second base. She slides into second base, barely making it.

Tiffany is grinning proudly. "Miss Gracie, I wonder if she can catch?"

The girl on first base is actually better in the outfield, so Leah takes first base. I nod to one of our best hitters.

I have a really good feeling about this. I look at Tiffany, giving her the go-ahead. Tiffany throws a fast pitch. I am still in awe of how good she is at pitching.

Daisy hits the ball. One of the outfielders catches it and throws it to Leah. The throw is a bit wild.

Leah keeps one leg on the base, and she practically does a freaking split and catches the ball. I blink for a few seconds before all the girls run to her, excited. I am so happy for her. I think she is going to be a star, just like Tiffany. We will go even further now. We were really good, but now we'll be even better.

Reid is asleep, lying on my shoulder. Aiden is still beside me, his hand on my back. I am growing to love having him by my side.

Amelia walks up to me. "She is really good."

"She is. She and Tiffany together are a force to be reckoned with."

Amelia nods.

All the girls have welcomed Leah with open arms, and she is just beaming. I love seeing her so happy. She deserves that.

I wrap up practice as the bus pulls back into the lot. Leah gets all of her belongings together and walks over to me and Aiden. "Thank you again, Aiden."

"It's nothing, sweetheart."

She walks to the bus and, with every step, she loses a bit more pep in her step.

"She doesn't want to go home," Aiden says, voicing my thoughts.

"No, she doesn't." My voice is barely above a whisper. My heart is hurting at the thought of what she's going to be walking into.

I feel Reid stirring in my arms, and I look down at him. "I'm surprised he slept like this."

Aiden runs his finger over Reid's chubby cheek. "I can't say I blame him." Aiden winks.

I shake my head, grinning, and pull Reid higher up on my shoulder.

"Do you want to come over to the house?" Aiden asks. "I will make dinner."

I freeze, my thoughts immediately going to *what if this and that happens.*

Stop, Gracie! I chastise myself. If I start going into my head, I will never get out. I decide to throw caution to the wind. "I would like that."

Nerves are hitting me full force. I have to stop myself from biting my nails, which is a horrible habit. When I get stressed, I instantly start nibbling on my finger or lip. Don't get me wrong. I am very excited to be around him. I really like Aiden. He's absolutely amazing. I just have these random thoughts sometimes.

"Do you want to follow me to the house?" he asks, studying me.

"Yeah." I smile and breathe deeply, finally controlling myself.

He pushes a stray hair out of my face and gently strokes his thumb across my cheekbone.

"You're a sweetie." I touch the back of his hand, which is resting on my face. His hand falls, our fingers intertwining.

"Remember what I said about that?" he says, pretending to scold me.

"Mhm."

I hold Reid while Aiden puts everything back into his truck. I take the time to stare at him without being caught.

I know one thing: right off the bat I felt safe around him. But he is a bad boy—I don't know one girl who doesn't want one of those.

He turns around and takes Reid from me. I instantly want him back. Why do I already feel such an attachment to this baby? "I'm going to go get into my car," I tell Aiden.

"Be safe." He kisses me tenderly on the side of my head, and I touch the spot he kissed, smiling.

I follow him to his house jamming out to Killswitch Engage—that is my weakness. I am a metalhead and there's no cure for it.

I pull in beside him and walk over to the truck; without thinking I take Reid out of his car seat. Aiden is leaning against my car, watching me. "I love seeing you with him."

Reid is sucking on his little fingers. "Anytime you need a babysitter, I am more than willing." I have always loved kids. I have always wanted to be a mom. That's one of my biggest goals in life. I want at least five.

I have honestly been thinking about adopting. I am not married, but I don't know if that will ever happen for me. I'm going to be completely honest—dating has not been at the forefront of my mind. I'd kind of given it up altogether, but Aiden just came out of nowhere.

"You got it, babe." His face is soft as he stares at both of us. I clear my throat and give Aiden Reid's pacifier; he's getting a bit fussy.

"So what are you feeding me for dinner?" I ask, bumping my hip into his as we walk into his house. Well, I actually bumped his thigh.

Walking into his house for the first time, my first thought is *it's absolutely beautiful*. The gorgeous cedar wood just takes my breath away.

You can tell right off the bat that a man lives here, but what makes it different is Reid's stuff intertwined with the house.

Aiden walks into the kitchen and takes a few steaks out of the refrigerator. Why do I have a feeling he had this preplanned?

"Do you want me to feed Reid?" I nod in the direction of the baby food; he is getting fussy.

"If you don't mind."

I put Reid in his high chair, and Aiden hands me the baby food and a spoon. "Are you hungry?" I coo to Reid.

His little arms are moving all over the place, and his legs are kicking with excitement. "You are just precious, sweet boy." I feed him his first bite. I know Aiden is staring at us, but in this moment it's just me and Reid.

I hear Aiden put something on the counter, and I look over and see him taking out the pan for the steaks.

"You always wanted to be a mom. Well, you did when we were younger."

I laugh. "I can't believe you remember that." That was so long ago.

Aiden winks at me. "I remember a lot about you."

I snort at his suggestive remark. We never did anything; I haven't done anything at all.

Yeah, you heard that right: I haven't had sex. I was way too young when I was with Aiden and, since then, relationships haven't been that great for me. That's a long story and, honestly, I don't want to think about that right now.

Once Reid is finished eating, I take him out of his high chair and into my lap. We both watch Aiden cook. Just the movement of him flipping the steaks is mouthwatering, because his muscles and the veins on the insides of his arms move.

He is just so freaking gorgeous.

"Your daddy is absolutely gorgeous, Reid," I whisper to him and he blows a raspberry at me, flashing that slobbery smile.

"Thank you," Aiden says without looking at me.

I stare at him, dumbfounded. How did he hear me? I feel my face heat, and I know it is red.

"Do you know how absolutely beautiful you are, CiCi? The way you are with those kids at the center and Reid?" He shakes his head for a second, his face softening as he studies me. "You're fucking beautiful, every part of you."

I am floored, completely speechless. My eyes start to burn from unshed tears. No one has ever said anything like that to me before. Without a word I set Reid into his swing and clip him in. Aiden is leaning against the counter, and I walk over and hug him, resting my head on his chest. He wraps his arms around me with his head resting on top of mine. "I don't know what to say." I look up at him.

He smiles, cupping my jaw. "There's nothing to say. I'm just being completely honest."

"Still, thank you." I really don't know how to react. I am not used to compliments because, honestly, I have been alone for a long time.

I know one thing for sure: I am in trouble. For the first time in a long time, I am hopeful—and completely terrified. I am going to stay out of my head and just live in the moment. I am going to put my trust in him. That is something that I don't give lightly, and I am going to give it to him.

AIDEN WALKS BACK DOWN the stairs, carrying a baby monitor. He just laid Reid down for the night, and I am sitting on the couch watching TV.

"Do you still like scary movies?" he asks as he sits beside me.

"I love them."

He turns on a new scary movie that I have been wanting to watch, *Annabelle*. *What do I do now? Oh my goodness, Gracelyn, stop being so weird over everything!*

There's a blanket on the back of the couch, and Aiden pulls it down. "Come here, CiCi."

I move closer to him until I am lying with my head against his chest, and he covers me with the blanket. This is absolute heaven. I close my eyes and bask in the feeling of being held.

I am wearing a sweater, and my hair is in a ponytail. He drags his fingers up my arm to my hair and pulls out my hair bow. His fingers start rubbing my scalp. Did I say heaven a minute ago? This is beyond that.

"Oh my," I manage to get out, and I put my hand on his stomach. I can feel his abs through his shirt. He continues to do this for around thirty minutes, and it's bliss. I look up at him, smiling. "You better be careful, I won't want to leave," I say jokingly.

He arches an eyebrow. "Is that supposed to be a bad thing?"

Well, that shuts me up.

His eyes go to my lips, then my body, which trembles because I know what's going to happen.

I lick my lips and he presses his lips to mine, oh so softly. I scoot a little closer and press my hand to his cheek. He takes over the kiss, but it's a kiss unlike any I have ever had before. He is so sweet and tender, and it's deep, passionate, and just out of this world.

My nerves are gone in that second, as I am taken into another world that is just me and Aiden. He buries his hand in my hair before running it down to the back of my neck. I almost freeze; then he moves it to my back.

A few minutes pass, and we both pull back and look each other in the eyes. "That was the best kiss I've ever had," I confess.

He gives me that smile that makes my stomach flip over. "I'm fucking lucky, nothing can ever compare to you." Just when he couldn't be any sweeter, he kisses my forehead and tucks me back into his chest. He wraps both arms around me. It's almost protective, and I have to admit I love it.

A couple of hours later

I wake up to a dark room, and I'm instantly panicked, not realizing where I am. Then I look over, seeing Aiden fast asleep.

I cover my face, embarrassed by my foolishness. We both fell asleep on the couch.

Aiden stirs beside me. "We fell asleep." He yawns and looks at his phone—it's two o'clock in the morning; we've been asleep for a couple of hours. "Do you want to stay the night? I don't want you traveling late at night like this."

At first I want to argue but, without thinking, I nod. He takes my hand and leads me up the stairs. I try not to read too much into it, but I can't help but wonder, *what if he wants more?*

He leads me into his bedroom, walks into his closet, and comes out with some clothes. He hands me a pair of sweats and a shirt. "This will be more comfortable."

I slip into the bathroom and change. I look at myself in the mirror; then I spot some face wash on the counter and I wash my face. I can't sleep if I have makeup on.

With one last look in the mirror, I step out into the bedroom with Aiden. I can't help but be a little nervous. I've never stayed all night with a guy before.

Aiden is lying in bed, leaning over the side, putting his phone on charge. I walk across the room, pull back the covers, and slide in.

Aiden hooks an arm around my belly and pulls me over until he is wrapped around me, spooning. I feel his fingers at the side of my neck as he pushes my hair over my shoulder. "Good night, Gracie," he whispers into my ear and kisses my cheek.

"Lights off," he says and the lights turn off in the bedroom.

"Good night, Aiden. I've had an amazing day," I whisper back. He squeezes me slightly. "Me too, angel."

I close my eyes and fall asleep.

6

I WAKE UP TO THE SOUND OF CRYING. I LOOK AT THE CLOCK ON THE nightstand; it's four o'clock in the morning.

I peek over my shoulder at Aiden, who is still asleep. Reid is whining rather than crying. I sit up and slowly crawl out of bed so I don't wake Aiden. I am sure doing this all alone is completely exhausting.

Reid's room is right next to Aiden's, and a nightlight projects stars across the ceiling. I look into the crib, and Reid stops crying the second he sees me. "You want to be cuddled? I bet you're hungry." I reach inside and pick him up.

His little fists grip my shirt, and his head rests on my shoulder. I carry him down the stairs and into the kitchen, where Aiden has his formula and bottles.

I prepare his bottle and carry him back upstairs to his room. A rocking chair in there is calling my name.

Sitting down, I give him his bottle. He looks up at me, and it's like my entire world just stops. His eyes are on mine; he's so precious and innocent. I just want to protect him from everything.

I start singing under my breath, rocking him.

Little by little, his eyes start to drift closed and, little by little, a piece of my heart belongs to Reid.

Aiden

She thought I was asleep, but I just wanted to see what she would do. One part of me knew she would, but seeing her in action, taking care of my son without a second thought, has me speechless.

Seeing the way she is with him fucking touches me. Actions speak much louder than words and I know, deep down, she was put back into my life for a reason.

And that is to be mine.

She gets up to put him back in his crib, and I hurry back to bed so she doesn't know.

Gracie

I wake up the next morning to the smell of breakfast. I roll over. Aiden's side of the bed is cold.

I scoot out of bed and walk down the stairs. Reid is sitting in a bouncer playing with some toys. "How are you this morning?" I touch his chubby cheek, and he grins at me.

I walk into the kitchen; Aiden is making breakfast. I lean against the doorjamb, watching him. He is shirtless, wearing only a pair of sweatpants. The sight of his back muscles moving has me salivating.

He turns around and sees me, and his smile is immediate. Without a second thought I walk over to him and hug him, my head resting on his warm chest.

I could get used to this, waking up every day and seeing this view. I lean my head back and he kisses me softly, causing tingles to run up my spine.

"Hmm, what an amazing thing to wake up to." I wink, running my hand down his side.

He studies my face for a minute before he kisses my forehead. I love getting forehead kisses; it's different and it's a gesture full of respect. There's a huge difference between the way my exes treated me and the way Aiden treats me. Aiden respects me.

I've had issues with one ex in particular. He has anger problems, and for a while it seemed he was everywhere that I went. Luckily, it's been months since I have seen him.

"Do you need my help with anything?" I ask.

"You can feed Reid if you want." He points to a bowl of oatmeal.

"I can do that." I walk into the living room and take Reid out of his bouncer and to his high chair.

"Da da da," he says between chewing on his fist. Aiden comes into a view in a split second. "Did he just say that?" he asks, his eyes lit up with pure happiness.

"He did."

He takes Reid out of my arms and starts pestering kisses all over his face. "That's my boy." His body moves side to side as he rocks Reid.

This is the one of the most beautiful moments I have ever seen. I wish that I'd had a father like this. My life would have been so much different. Vomit starts crawling up my throat.

Don't go there, Gracelyn.

"Say da da," Aiden says. Reid opens and closes his mouth like he is trying. "That's okay, my boy." Aiden kisses his cheek and settles him in his high chair.

When I don't think that Aiden could get any more attractive, he goes and does something like this, completely changing my mind.

"What are your plans today?" he asks as he flips some pancakes on the stove.

I shrug before answering. "No plans today."

He takes out a couple of plates. "Yes, you do."

"What do you mean?"

"You have plans with me." He gives me a *duh* look and I laugh. He can be so cheesy sometimes, but I like that. I just like him.

He brings over my plate.

"You didn't have to make me breakfast." I'm not used to someone doing things for me.

"It's nothing, sweetheart." He rubs my back sweetly before sitting next to me at the table.

I feed Reid his oatmeal, enjoying watching all of the little faces he makes. He slams his hand down on the tray, spraying oatmeal everywhere. Aiden laughs and I join in, wiping off my arm and cleaning up Reid as best as I can before continuing to feed him.

"You should have seen me and him the first time I fed him baby food. It was a disaster."

I get the visual of a big badass biker covered in baby food, and I burst out laughing. "I can see that now."

"Tonight do you want to go to a bar? A few of my brothers in the MC and their old ladies will be there."

I think for a few seconds; do I want to do this? I decide to just go for it. "Yeah, I would like that. I need to head home first so I can change and get ready."

"That's fine. Mom is babysitting Reid tonight. She has been bugging me for days." I always loved his mother; she is the kind of mother you dream of. She bakes you cookies, takes you to all your games, and takes care of you when you're sick.

I had none of that.

It got to the point that I went years without a hug or any kind of affection from my family.

I have been through a lot. It hasn't made me bitter, but I am very cautious about whom I let in my life, because I don't want to get hurt.

WE WALK into a bar I have been to a couple of times with a few of my friends. Apparently, the club owns it, like the rest of the town.

He is holding my hand as he leads me inside, and quite a few eyes are on us as we move through the place. I notice many Grim Sinners vests and a few other MC vests throughout the place; it's a biker bar so it's fitting.

The bar is filled with a smoky haze, with a blue-tinted light shining through the building. The tabletops are wood, giving off a rustic country feel.

Lane and Amelia are sitting at one of the tables. I'm excited to see Amelia outside of practices and games.

"Hi, Gracie. I'm so glad you came!" She hops off her high-top chair and gives me a hug. I let go of Aiden's hand so I can hug her back.

She puts her arm around me and, with her free hand, she points at Lane. "You know Lane, but the guy next to him is Wilder. His vice president." I smile and nod at him.

She points to the guy on the other side of Lane. "That is Travis. He is a member of the club, and the guy next to him is Trenton. He grew up in the club with Lane and Wilder." She then proceeds to introduce the women.

"It's nice to meet all of y'all."

Aiden presses his hand to my back; it's like he is letting me know he is here. "Oh yeah, the guy walking toward us right now is the newest member, Logan."

I turn around and the first thing I think is *huge and scary*. This man is covered in tattoos, right up to his chin. His hair and eyes are dark brown, he has a beard, and a scar reaches from his bottom lip to his cheekbone. That makes him look way scarier.

"It's nice to meet you, Logan."

He smiles, which I didn't expect one bit because he just doesn't look like a smiler. "It's nice to meet you, Grace." He reaches forward and shakes my hand, which completely disappears in his grip.

He walks around me and to the bar. I guess he is not a man of many words. Aiden leads me to Lane and Amelia, never leaving my side. Usually I am very anxious in crowded places, but I feel safe.

Aiden bends down to whisper in my ear. "Do you want something to drink?"

"No, thank you. I don't drink." I got a drink, of course, when I turned twenty-one because it's a rite of passage, but honestly I am too afraid. I want to make sure I am always aware of my surroundings and those around me.

"Okay." His hand drifts from my back to the back of my neck, comforting me. It's like he knows that I have anxiety. I know it's not a big deal, but I don't want to disappoint him. I really like him, and I am afraid that something might happen then, poof, he is out of my life.

Stop the thoughts, Gracelyn.

At times I fight a war in my head. It's like I have two sides. Without thinking I back up and press myself into Aiden's side.

He looks over at me for a second before shooting me that oh-so-sexy wink.

Amelia brings me out of my Aiden fog. "Tiffany was majorly excited that Leah joined the team."

"I am so glad that they are getting along. I think these girls are going to go far."

Amelia's eyes light up. "I think so too. We will make sure their dreams are accomplished. I do dread when she ages out."

I have thought of that myself. My softball team is a little different. Students from any school can join; it's more of an elite team. "Maybe I will just keep the same girls forever, until they are in college," I tease and she laughs, but if I could do it I would. I love my girls. Many of them are from not-so-great circumstances, but they have so much talent and drive. I want to see them all thrive.

One of the old ladies, Bailey, walks over to me. "How did you and Aiden meet?" She looks at us with a shit-eating grin.

"It's a long story."

Joslyn, Wilder's old lady, takes my hand and pulls me away from Aiden. We ladies get our own table, and they all lean forward, their eyes shining with excitement.

I explain to them how I had major road rage and, at the spur of the moment, I complimented him; how he showed up at the game; and how, on date night, we found out we'd been together at fourteen.

"Oh wow," Bailey says, staring at me wide eyed.

"It's fate," Joslyn says, holding her chest. One by one, they nod in agreement.

"You guys are beautiful standing next to each other," Amelia says.

My heart warms at these beautiful, kind ladies. "Thank you so much. You guys are so sweet.

"Just being truthful."

I end up having an amazing night, spending time with these girls. I have had female friends, but these girls make me feel like I could really trust them. Most of Aiden's friends are such genuine people. It makes me think that the world isn't as shitty as I thought.

It's easy to become jaded, especially when terrible things happen. Then you meet amazing people, and it restores your faith in humanity.

"Well, great."

I follow Joslyn's eyes and see a man stumbling in our direction. Well, mostly in my direction. One second he's close to me, and the next Aiden is standing next to me, stopping the guy in his tracks.

He looks at Aiden before he backs away and crosses the room.

My mouth is hanging open at this point, because that was hot as hell.

Aiden touches the back of my head before kissing my temple, and he goes back to his friends.

I look at the girls wide eyed because that just happened, but they aren't shocked like I am. "Welcome to the world of alphas, honey. They are a different but amazing breed."

I wholeheartedly agree. I think this is going to be an entirely different kind of experience, and that is something I am excited about.

I am excited about him. My eyes connect with his and, for the first time in a long time, it's like I am finally living.

7

GRACE

AFTER BEING OUT UNTIL AROUND TWO O'CLOCK IN THE MORNING, I decided to stay all night with Aiden. Honestly, I just wanted to fall asleep in his arms again.

I look at the clock on the wall, wondering what brought me out of my sleep, and that's when my phone starts ringing again. It's seven o'clock in the morning. I never get a call at this time.

I pick it up, sitting up in bed, trying not to wake Aiden. "Hello?" I whisper.

"Is this Gracelyn Walters?" a professional-sounding lady asks, and my stomach sinks. I don't think this is going to be good.

"Yes?" I feel the bed move and, from the corner of my eye, I see Aiden sit up, confused.

"I am calling about your aunt Mary. She is on life support at the ICU in Saint Thomas. If you want to come see her, I would come as soon as possible."

"Thank you," I whisper back. I put the phone down, and I'm instantly hit with *what do I do?*

My dad's side of the family and I just don't get along. I did like Aunt Mary, but she was the only one. The rest of my dad's family aren't good people, and I want to avoid them like the plague. I have not seen my dad or any of his family since I was eleven years old.

But I want to see my aunt.

"Sweetheart, are you okay?" Aiden pulls me into his lap and turns my face gently so I am looking at him.

My stomach is in a bunch of knots; I am sick and confused. I am scared, because I don't want to see... "That was the hospital. My aunt is on life support, and they called the family in."

His face softens. "Let's get dressed and I will drive you there."

Relief hits me. "You're going with me?"

He touches the side of my face, his thumb stroking my cheekbone so tenderly. "Of course I am."

I feel like I should tell him about that side of the family. The anxiety is clawing up my throat, making it hard to breathe. I close my eyes, trying not to think about...

"I have to warn you, I have not seen that side of the family since I was eleven years old. They aren't nice people."

"Don't worry, baby, I will be right by your side."

Relief slams into me hard. I never realized how much I needed to hear that and know that I am not going into this alone.

I grip the sides of his face, kissing him softly. I want this kiss to let him know every single thing I am feeling.

We kiss for a few minutes before pulling away, and I press one last kiss on his cheek. I slide out of bed and into the bathroom. Luckily, I was smart enough to pack an overnight bag.

I hurry and get dressed because I just want to get this over with. I want to see her, pay my respects, and just get the hell out.

I stop putting foundation on my face and look at myself in the mirror. *You got this, Gracelyn. You aren't the same little girl anymore. You are strong and brave, and you can handle every single thing life throws at you.*

I immediately feel better. I square my shoulders and walk out of the bathroom, ready as I ever will be.

AIDEN HITS the elevator button for me. I swallow hard in anticipation of what I'm going to face. I can feel him looking at me.

"It's fucking killing me to see you so anxious. Want me to just clear everyone out so you can see her alone?" He pulls me into a hug.

I laugh. "That would be so appreciated but unnecessary. You're a sweetheart." I look up at him, smiling.

His eyes are shining with happiness, and he presses his lips to mine. "I told you I wasn't sweet," he says under his breath.

"Keep telling yourself that," I tease, just as the door opens, bringing me back to reality. He takes my hand, and I squeeze his in thanks. I am beyond thankful I am not doing this alone.

I walk into the ICU, and the first thing I notice is my aunt. Aunt Mary is one of my dad's sisters. Other members of my dad's family are gathered in the ICU. I want to turn around and run out of the room. I just pray that the two people I hate more than anything aren't here.

I gather my strength and walk toward them with my head held high. They only have the amount of power over me that I give them.

I am not a small child anymore; it's different now.

My aunt Glenna looks up at me, and her husband, Ron, is right behind her, sitting in a chair. She scowls at me, looking me up and down. "I'm sorry but only family are allowed in here."

That immediately pisses me right off. "Did you forget you had a niece?"

Her eyes widen as she takes a closer look at me. She looks way different than she used to. Over the years, life has not been easy for her; the cut on her lip is a sign of that. When you're involved with this family, a rough life is inevitable.

Most of the men in the family have little to no sympathy for anyone. They just do whatever satisfies them, even when it hurts others. Hurting others is something they take great pride in. They love and thrive on it.

"Gracelyn?" Aunt Glenna says as I walk through the entrance. One by one, my relatives look at me, shocked.

"How did you know?" Aunt Glenna says and I can tell, right off the bat, she is angry.

Did I mention they hated me?

I ignore all of them; it's like my skin is crawling. The bathroom door opens and someone walks out. I immediately feel sick to my stomach. I look into the eyes of my dad's brother. His eyes connect with mine, and I want to scream.

I look away and walk to the edge of Aunt Mary's bed, ignoring the stares and the whispering.

Aunt Mary looks so lifeless. I got out of this family, but she didn't. I knew she hated it, but she got married when she was just fourteen or fifteen. This life was all she had known.

She tried to make her world normal, to separate herself from the insanity, but it always bleeds into you one way or another.

My heart breaks for her because not once did she experience peace. She never had one ounce of happiness with her husband. She wouldn't have known what love was. And she didn't have kids because she couldn't bring one into the world she was living in.

I bend down and kiss her cheek and touch her hand. "I am so sorry. May you finally have the peace you always dreamt of, Mary. I hope that you're laughing and happy," I whisper in her ear, my heart breaking for her.

She was the only sense of normal I ever had in my life. She always made sure, one way or another, that I had everything I needed. She tried her best; she tried to protect me.

She is the closest thing I ever had to family.

A tear slips down my cheek, and I push her hair away from her face. She is so pale. I wish I could have talked to her one more time and let her know the world is better outside of hell.

"I think it's time for you to go." I tense at the sound of my uncle's voice, and disgust settles in my stomach.

"Why don't you mind your own fucking business," Aiden snarls. This is the first time in my life someone has stood up for me.

"I love you." I kiss the top of Mary's head one last time, and I look at the room filled with people who hate me. I want to say so much to them, but it's not worth it. Aiden puts his hand on the small of my back. He went into a war zone with me, and he stood right by my side and faced them down. I will never, ever forget that.

We start to walk out of the room, and my uncle steps toward me. A second later my world stops on its axis as the next person steps into the room.

I want to scream; the pain is so fierce it pierces my stomach and heart. I can't breathe. I am frozen in complete, utter panic.

The memories hit me full force.

My father recognizes me, and he looks me up and down. I want to throw up.

Aiden

I can tell that Grace is hurt by what's happened to her aunt. I can feel the hate pouring off the people in the room, and I want to fucking give them a piece of my mind. She doesn't need this shit. She is fucking beautiful, and these people are the exact opposite.

I can feel the bitterness and meanness written all fucking over them. Especially the fucker who walked out of the bathroom and glared at her.

I stepped in front of her. If he is going to glare at someone, it's going to be me. Not her.

Grace steps away from her aunt and looks at everyone in the room, then at the guy who's been glaring at her, and she pales. I put my hand on her back, my body stiffening, ready to beat some ass.

Someone walks into the room, and his eyes immediately go to Grace. She sucks in a sharp breath and her face pales, her whole body shaking under my touch.

What the fuck is going on?

I step in front of her, and she grips the back of my shirt, burying her face into my back like she wants to hide. The man who just stepped into the room moves closer to Grace. "What the fuck is she doing here?"

The one who came out of the bathroom speaks up. "I don't know, but she needs to leave or she's going to fucking regret it."

I snap.

I grip him by his fucking throat, slamming him into the bathroom door. His head bounces off the door, causing his eyes to roll back for a second. "I don't know who you are, but threatening her is a deadly fucking mistake. Watch your back." I wish I could put a bullet in his head.

I let him go and he collapses to the ground. I put my arm around Grace. She holds onto me tightly, like she is afraid of being ripped away.

We step out into the hallway. The man whose head I just slammed into a door follows us out of the room. "It's very good to see you again."

She doesn't turn around or acknowledge him but pulls me down the hallway and into the elevator. Once inside, she leans against the wall and stares at the ceiling like she is in a daze.

I am fucking worried.

Grace

I don't remember how I got outside. I don't remember anything but the words of my father, saying it was good to see me.

I had a moment of pure, utter terror, and the panic attack

completely took over. If Aiden hadn't been there, I don't know what could've happened.

My worst nightmare came to life: my father and uncle in the same room.

Hands grip my face, and I look into Aiden's eyes. I can tell he is worried. "Grace, what's the matter?"

My stomach turns, and I run to the back of the truck and vomit on the grass. I hear him open the truck, and then he is there with me. He pulls my hair out of my face, takes the hair tie off my wrist, and pulls my hair into a bun. "Here." Baby wipes come into view, and he presses one against the back of my neck, cooling me.

Why has he not run?

I clean my face; then he hands me a small bottle of mouthwash and I rinse out my mouth. He helps me into his truck and gets in on the driver's side. Then he looks at me and I look down in my lap.

What do I say?

"Sweetheart, it's fucking killing me knowing you're so upset, and I don't know what's going on."

I close my eyes and try not to burst into tears. If I tell him, this might be the very last time I am around him. But I also have to be true to myself and not pretend that everything is perfect, because it's far from it.

"What do you want to know?" I whisper, slightly heartbroken.

"Everything.

"Let's go back to your house and I will tell you." I lean against the door and just try to hold myself together, expecting the worst outcome.

We reach his house way too soon. I just want to scream at the injustice of it all.

I walk into his house, without bothering to look at him, and sit down on his couch. I grab the blanket off the back, covering myself.

I see his feet first; then I feel the couch shift as he sits beside me. I make myself look at him, and his face turns blurry as my eyes fill with tears.

"I am so afraid," I whisper. I have only told my story to a few people, and one of them is my therapist.

He intertwines our fingers. "No matter what, I will be here with you."

If only... This is so embarrassing.

"I was three years old when the abuse started. It started small. It started with touches." I stop as I remember to breathe. I can't look at him, so I look at the ground and just try to hold myself together, because telling him is probably the hardest thing I have ever done.

"My father made it seem like it was normal, then it got worse —until he raped me. He raped me for years, until I was around eleven years old, but before that it got worse." A sob escapes because the pain of it all is coming back.

"I just remember praying, as a child, begging for it all to stop. My dad's side of the family knew it was happening." I grip my blanket, just hoping it can keep me grounded until I can get it all out. "So much happened—physical, sexual, and verbal abuse was my everyday life. Then one day my uncle started touching me, and then I realized I needed to get out."

I sniff. *Please help me, Lord, help me have the strength.*

"One day I made my father take me to the doctor because I knew that was the only time I could get privacy. I was home-schooled and just completely trapped. I told her everything, and the police were called right then and there. My father and uncle were arrested, and then I became the person everyone on my dad's side of the family hated. Today was the first time I have seen them since I was eleven years old, when I testified."

I am picked up off the couch and set on his lap. I look at him for the first time since I started telling him.

"It fucking hurts me, baby, that this happened to you. You're so fucking brave, putting a stop to it. You're the most amazing, beautiful woman. I am in awe of your strength." He kisses my forehead, and that's all it takes for me to break.

I sob. I cry for the first time in a long time, but these tears are healing; they're releasing all of the bad.

He holds me—he lets me get rid of all the pain—and I can't tell you how many times I have wanted this to happen.

"I thought you wouldn't want me anymore," I tell him.

He looks at me like I'm crazy. "That's not possible, baby. There's absolutely nothing wrong with you. You're fucking perfect. This shit doesn't define you. It shows how unbelievably strong you are." He wipes my tears away with his thumb. "Nothing can change the way I see you. You're my CiCi."

For the first time today, I smile—because a huge part of me just fell in love with Aiden.

I lay my head on his shoulder and, for the first time in my life, I let myself be held and comforted.

Aiden

I never expected her to tell me that. I knew shit had happened, but I never imagined that happened to her.

She is so fucking beautiful, filled with such light and happiness, that I never thought. Hearing what happened to her fucking killed me right down to my soul. I was in the presence of those fuckers earlier, and if I had known, they would have had bullets in their heads right then.

They will pay. Every single fucking person who had a hand in what happened to her. If they caused her an ounce of pain, they will face the wrath of me.

I know one fucking thing. I will make sure she never suffers any amount of pain in her life again, and I will never see the fear of rejection in her eyes—that shit hurt.

I see her in a whole new fucking light. I'm filled with so much respect because she has kept on going—and look what she is doing with her life.

She is fucking amazing. She is an angel. She is not bitter or mad at the world; that shows what kind of person she is.

She is my person.

She is mine.

Nothing can change that. This shit will be dealt with, and she will never have to be afraid of them again.

"Sleep, baby," I tell her softly, stroking her back and holding her. I don't think I could let her go if I tried.

This has ripped my fucking heart open. I am so fucking mad, but I can't let her see that. She needs me, and I am going to be whatever she needs. Right now she needs me to be calm and comforting, and that's what she's going to get.

Their day will come.

Aiden

Grace left earlier to go to the center, and I am going to the club. I have to take care of those fuckers that hurt her.

I am so fucking pissed; it's just gotten worse every single second since she told me. The fear on her face when she saw both of them in the same room fucking killed me.

It's hard to believe she went through all this alone. When we were fourteen years old, I noticed a change in her. I knew she was going through some stuff, but I had no idea what she was struggling with.

In the clubhouse, Lane is sitting at the bar with Travis, Wilder, Smiley, and Lucas.

"Can I speak to you guys?" I nod in the direction of the room where we have our meetings. I hold the door open for them as they walk inside. Then I shut the door and close my eyes for a second, because I have to tell them of the horrors Grace has experienced.

I sit down and stare at the table before me. I can feel their eyes on me, but where do I fucking begin?

I know this is her story, and she confided in me. But I need my brothers in this, because I am going to be getting revenge and they have to be prepared for the blowback.

I start from the beginning, with the phone call about her aunt dying; then I move from her being so fucking terrified to her telling me everything.

I don't want to think about what would have happened if I hadn't been there. They fucking hated her because most of them went to jail, but I am so proud of her.

"Fuckkkk." Lane slams his hand on the table. I tighten my fists, wanting more than anything to choke the life out of her father.

Do you think I will let him die easily?

He is going to suffer. She suffered for years, and he is going to feel that, but ten times worse.

I rub my hand over my face and lean back in my seat looking at the others. They are just as pissed off as I am.

"I say we start with her aunt Glenna and her husband, then her uncle who tried to do shit to her, and then him." I can't even say his name.

"I say we get the girls in on the aunt, shall we?" Lane grins at all of us, and I laugh because that will be epic.

Smiley finally says something. "I think we need to have a family barbecue so Grace can be introduced to the others. She and Adeline would have a lot in common."

I nod. His woman went through years of hell with her husband—different circumstances but still, no matter what, this shouldn't happen.

Lane takes out his phone and starts texting. I know he is getting this ball rolling. "It's time for some fuckers to get what they deserve."

A COUPLE OF HOURS LATER, a shit ton of people pile into the club-house. Amelia and Bailey show up first, pissed off, then Shaylin walks in with Kayla, Jean, Alisha, and Paisley, and their men are right behind them.

It seems the two clubs are coming together for this. I grin at everyone, especially Shaylin, who walked in carrying her base-ball bat. She is the female version of Smiley. I saw her kick some-one's ass and smile the whole time like it was the most fun thing in the world.

The door flies open again, and Konrad, Maverick, Walker, and Trenton step inside. Lane steps forward. "Many of you here know what Aiden told us about what happened to his woman. This shit is unforgivable. Before she became Aiden's woman, she was already family. She is Tiffany's softball coach, and we have become close to her."

My heart fills with love for my brothers; this is family. I grew up just having my mother. She had gotten pregnant with me when she was sixteen years old, and she did everything she could do to give me a good life.

"We are going to her aunt and uncle's today. They didn't have a direct hand in her abuse but, from what she has told me, they actually witnessed it but they didn't stop it. In my eyes they are just as guilty."

I cannot fucking fathom the shit she has dealt with. No one had her back besides the aunt who is on life support right now, and she was as much of a victim in many ways.

I read Mary's chart while Grace was whispering to her, and I learned that she had blunt force trauma to her head and internal bleeding. My guess is that he hurt her. Her husband is the man who tried to touch Gracelyn before she told the cops what had happened to her.

"This stays among ourselves." I eye everyone in the room, and they all nod.

"Let's ride."

We file out of the clubhouse and head toward the aunt and uncle. We are starting with the smallest offenses, so her father will know we are fucking coming for him.

My hands are fucking burning to be wrapped around his neck and watch the life leave his eyes. I grit my teeth, riding side by side with Travis, and stare straight ahead. My body is ready for this.

The second we hit the outskirts of town, I know exactly where we are going. We are going to a trailer park where violence and drugs run rampant.

Lane pulls to a stop in front of a beaten-down trailer. The porch is barely connected to the house, and plastic covers the broken windows. The door does not even fully cover the doorway.

I get off my bike. The door is pried open, and out step Glena and her husband, Richard. Her eyes are wide as she takes in everyone before her gaze settles on me. "What is the meaning of this?" she screeches in a godawful voice.

Richard looks like he is about to piss himself. He is standing behind his wife, and that's a bitch move. If you don't protect your woman, then you're a low piece of shit.

"You." She points her finger in my direction dramatically, and I smirk in amusement at her trying to be brave. "What do you want? I see the bitch isn't here with you."

I see fucking red.

"Get your fucking asses off that dilapidated porch. Gracelyn has informed me of what went on."

They pale and start to back up toward the house.

Like that shit is going to stop us from getting inside.

"We didn't do shit to her!" Richard has finally gotten a voice and screamed at all of us, which isn't helping his cause.

I take a step closer to them. "Yeah, but you didn't do shit to stop it either, did you?"

That leaves them silent. I motion for them to walk off their porch, and they do as we ask. Shaylin stands next to me, and the moment they step off the last step, I punch Richard hard in the face, knocking him on his ass.

That felt fucking amazing.

Shaylin laughs and grips Glenna's hair, and she drags her to the rest of the girls. Richard gets off the ground, and I take steps back to bring him closer to the others.

"Look, I never hurt her," he says. Glenna is making excuses too.

"Do you think that matters? You knew what was happening." I take a step closer, so I am looking down into his face. "You knew he was raping and beating her." I yell the last part.

He doesn't say anything, but he nods. That's all it takes for me to lose it. I punch him over and over in the face, and he falls to the ground. I feel his teeth breaking beneath my fist.

I bend over him and grip his jaw. "You don't need your mouth, you didn't speak up when you should have. You don't have that luxury anymore."

I take out my knife. Lucas pries his mouth open. Travis bends down beside me with some pliers, and he grips his tongue and pulls. I use my knife and cut part of his tongue off.

I slam his mouth shut and bend down next to his ear. "Enjoy not having a voice, she didn't have one. She suffered every single day for years, while you wallowed in your shit and enjoyed life, letting it fucking happen." I get up and spit on the ground next to him. Worthless piece of shit. He could have stopped it—she could have too—but they didn't.

Lane touches my shoulder. "He deserved it."

I look over at the women; they are taking turns bitch slapping her. I laugh loudly. "I think, ladies, she needs to be left alive. He will need a hospital."

Glenna looks up from the ground at her husband, and she glares at me.

"Don't say a fucking word, be thankful he's alive and so are you."

She nods and crawls over to Richard, who's choking on his blood.

We watch as they leave. "Man, that was fun," Shaylin says and we all burst out laughing, even Butcher.

I feel a little bit lighter, but I won't feel like I can fully breathe until her uncle has been dealt with and her father is dead.

I get on my bike. There's one thing on my mind, and that's to pick up Grace and go home to my boy.

8

GRACE

I AM NERVOUS. AIDEN TOLD ME THAT HIS MOTHER, LAURIE, WILL BE here any minute with Reid.

Did I mention I am nervous? No, it's more like I am terrified.

I want her to like me. I want her to accept me and think that I'm good for her son, because I am really starting to care for Aiden a lot and Reid has already stolen my heart.

When Aiden picked me up from the center, one part of me was afraid that he would treat me differently, but it's not like that at all.

One of my biggest fears is someone pitying me—I don't want that. Yes, horrible things happened to me, but I don't want that to define my life. It already took many years from me.

I want to be intimate with Aiden. I am absolutely terrified, but I want to take that chance—and live. I trust Aiden, unlike any of my other exes. He is different.

I hear the doorbell, and my heart jumps into my throat. I stand up as Aiden opens the door and his mother steps inside with Reid. She looks at me and then does a double take before she smiles. "Gracelyn?"

"It's me, Laurie."

She walks over to me and hugs me tightly. I want to cry because I have missed her, and her hugs are the best.

"I have thought about you so much over the years." She leans back and touches my cheeks, studying my face. "You were beautiful then, but now you're breathtaking." She pats my cheek softly.

Did I mention how sweet his mother is? She is one of the beautiful women I have ever seen and doesn't look her age. Not that she's that old. She had Aiden when she was just sixteen.

"You haven't changed one bit, Laurie, still a fox." I wink at her and she blushes, laughing.

"Stop that. I am a grandma now. I'm old."

I roll my eyes and look over at Aiden, who is pestering kisses all over Reid's face. He was chomping at the bit for Laurie to bring him.

"You're not and you know it," I scold her and she just waves off the compliment.

"Mom, we are having a barbecue at the clubhouse tomorrow evening, and I want you to come with me and Grace."

I smile at being included. He says *we* all the time, and I love that statement because it means that he anticipates my being around for a while.

"Sure, baby. What time?" She sits down on the couch, making herself at home.

Another thing I admire about her is her confidence. She carries herself in a way that I hope I can one day, and she's a momma bear right down to her bones.

"Six." Aiden brings me Reid.

"Hi, sweet boy." I hug him gently, kissing his forehead. I missed him too.

"Do I need to bring anything since it's my first time at the club?" Laurie takes her shoes off and curls up on the couch. Aiden invited her for dinner, and we are having a movie night. I love that he is including her. I know it means a lot to her, and it shows what an amazing person he is.

"No, everything is taken care of."

We hear a beeping sound, and Aiden pushes a button next to the door. "It's the pizza guy."

He steps out onto the porch, and I sit down next to Laurie. "I'm so glad you're back in my son's life." She touches my hand.

My poor heart can't handle all this; my eyes fill with tears. "Thank you. I am glad that he's back." I touch my heart; it's filled with so much happiness I feel like I can fly.

Reid takes the moment to start crying.

"What's the matter, sweetheart? Hungry?" I rock him slightly.

"He may be ready for a bottle. It's probably bedtime for him. I already bathed him," Laurie tells us.

I look at the clock and it's hitting eight. "Okay, let me fix him a bottle." I make his bottle with him on my hip, fussing the whole time, I sit down and cuddle him before he yanks the bottle to his mouth. I laugh and rub the back of his head.

"Better now, huh?" I look around the room. Aiden and Laurie are both staring at me. "What?" I ask and they give me identical smiles.

Aiden sits on the other side of me and opens the pizza. "Cheese or pepperoni?"

"Cheese."

He puts it on a plate and leans back. "Open."

I arch an eyebrow in confusion. "What are you doing?"

He laughs. "I'm going to feed you. You're taking care of my son, and I will take care of my CiCi."

Well, there goes my heart once again. So I let him feed me though I'm not used to this. I'm sure this is a common thing for a lot of people, but for me it's everything. I love that someone cares enough to take care of me. I am so used to taking care of others it's kind of nice to sit back and let it happen.

A couple of hours later, his mother leaves. I'm in Aiden's bathroom, brushing my teeth, trying not to overthink and be nervous. Because if I'm completely honest, I am terrified. I also know I am safe here, but the fear is in the back of my mind.

Stop thinking, Gracelyn. This is Aiden. He is not going to do anything to make you feel unsafe or comfortable.

I put on my big-girl panties and step out into the bedroom. He is sitting in bed staring at the TV on the wall next to the bathroom door.

I turn off the light and slowly walk over, his eyes on me with every step. I'm wearing one of his shirts and a pair of shorts. He pulls back the blanket, and I slide in next to him. He wraps his arm around me, pulling me against him until my face touches his warm shoulder. "Are you okay?" he asks.

I lean my head back and look at him. "Yeah, I'm fine. It was hard telling you, but I am glad that I did."

He gently pushes my hair behind my ear. "I'm glad you did too, CiCi. Your family will never fucking hurt you again. You're mine now. I have you." He kisses my forehead.

I clench my eyes closed, his words hitting me hard. How many times have I wanted to hear those words? So many times.

I open my eyes, the tears falling down my cheeks. His thumb catches them. "My Gracelyn," he whispers.

I close my eyes and kiss him, slowly testing the waters. I kiss him softly, butterflies completely swarming my belly.

He gently lays me down on the bed, leaning over me. My hands are shaking as I touch his shoulder.

At moments like this I wish I were normal.

His hands move down my sides and slide under my shirt, touching my belly, I jolt at the feeling of his hands.

One of the things I have noticed through the years is I'm afraid of physical intimacy because all I have known is pain.

I kiss him back harder, digging my fingers into his hair and stroking the side of his face, loving the feel of his jaw moving as he kisses me. His lips drift from my mouth to my cheek and then my neck. I stiffen because that's one of the places that freaks me out. I was choked many times. He stops kissing me and looks at me. "He hurt you here, didn't he?" he whispers.

I close my eyes, feeling ashamed. Why would someone want someone like me, who is so damaged?

"Baby... Don't ever turn your head in embarrassment. If you could only see yourself the way I see you, you wouldn't feel a single ounce of embarrassment." He touches the center of my neck with the tip of his finger. "Let me show you."

I nod and he drags his fingers along my neck, gently touching and rubbing, and little by little I relax. He studies my face before he kisses the side of my neck. I close my eyes and enjoy the feeling. I touch the back of his head and just let go.

I let out a large sigh without even thinking. I'm enjoying this way too much, and I'm growing wetter by the second.

His lips move down my neck to my collarbone, then my chest. I feel his hand touching the waistband of my shorts.

I open my eyes and look at him, and his eyes connect with mine, asking. I nod.

I lift my hips, helping him take off my shorts and underwear, leaving me completely bare to him.

"Gracelyn." He is looking at me in such a tender and beautiful way. "I would never hurt you, trust me." He whispers the last part.

"I trust you, Aiden." I touch the side of his face and, to show that I do, I sit up and take off my shirt. I don't have a bra on.

"I will fucking cherish your trust, baby. Let me love you. I know you're scared, I can see it in your eyes, but being afraid of me is something you never have to be. I will protect you, cherish you, and take care of you."

With the back of my hand, I wipe the tears off my face. I know I seem like such a baby, but being hurt by the person who is supposed to protect you more than any other— it hurts right to your core. I've been failed by so many people, and I expect it from everyone.

"I don't deserve you," I whisper, feeling this from the bottom of my heart.

He looks genuinely shocked. "Don't ever fucking say that. You deserve the fucking world, baby, and I plan on handing it to you."

That leaves me speechless.

He scoots down the bed, and I fall back down onto my back. I close my eyes and breathe, trying not to overthink.

He strokes my inner thighs, running down my legs and back up again. His lips touch me right below my belly button.

One of my hands is resting on my stomach; he intertwines our fingers and searches my face before he ducks his head.

I feel his warm breath before his tongue swipes my clit. All my worries go right out the window in a split second.

I open my legs wider, gripping his hand hard as he slowly teases me, and it's the most amazing feeling in the world.

I masturbate, like everyone in the world, but this is a whole different ballgame.

"That's right, sweetheart, feel, enjoy, and let me take care of you," he says softly.

I let go of his hand and grip the sheets by my sides, my body already stiffening. I feel his finger at my entrance before he slowly slides it inside me. I shiver all the way down to my legs, my toes curling.

"My baby liked that." He sucks my clit deep into his mouth. He wiggles his finger along with the movement of his tongue. Then he slowly adds another finger and curls it in a come hither motion that sets me off.

My legs stiffen, tightening around his head. I slowly loosen my thighs, and he rubs my legs and scoots up the bed to hold me.

This has changed my life. I knew that I shouldn't have been scared, but the little girl is still a part of me. I don't have to be afraid, but I don't think I would have made the plunge unless it was Aiden.

I'm feeling empowered. "I want to do more, if you want to," I tell him before I chicken out. I want to go the rest of the way. I need to.

He leans over me. "Baby, that was for you. You don't have to."

This is why I want to. He is thinking of me and making sure I'm okay. I touch the side of his face. "I want to. Love me, Aiden. Show me."

He closes his eyes, my words affecting him. I lean forward and kiss the side of his face, wrapping my arms around his neck.

He touches the side of my arm before his hand drifts to the back of my head. "Are you one hundred percent sure, Grace?"

"I'm ready. I want it to be you. I've never..." I stop because what am I? What do I call myself?

"You've never?".

"No, you're the first since..."

He grins so beautifully, stirring a deeper part of my heart. "I'm honored." He kisses me, oh so sweetly, and I can feel the passion.

"I'm clean and on birth control," I tell him when he starts to reach into the nightstand drawer.

"I'm clean too."

He slides off the bed, taking off his clothes. I eye him every moment, enjoying seeing him fully naked for the first time.

Nerves fill my stomach. But this time it's not the bad kind, but the anticipation of what's about to happen. Of course it's going to be uncomfortable, but I also know with Aiden it's going to be perfect no matter what.

I am doing a three sixty, but just letting go, letting it happen, and letting Aiden pleasure me made me change. I saw it as scary for such a long time. I never really wanted to be intimate with anyone, but with him it's so different. I want to throw caution to the wind and have that deeper connection with him.

He slides into bed with me, kissing me. He gets between my legs, and I rest my right leg on the back of his thigh. I can feel my heart starting to beat faster as the reality of what's about to happen kicks in.

His hand snakes between our bodies, and his finger strokes my clit in little circles. I hiss, breaking the kiss, because I'm really sensitive after my orgasm earlier.

He moves down my body, and his tongue runs across my nipple before sucking hard. My back rises from the bed.

"Is my baby ready for me?" he growls, moving to my other breast.

"Yes," I say, sounding completely out of breath.

"Fucking soaked," he hisses, dragging his tongue between my breasts. He makes his way up my body until his face is above mine. He cups my pussy. "Who does this belong to?" he asks.

"Me."

He grins goofily. "That's fucking right, baby, but it's mine to worship." He pulls my legs further apart, and I feel him at my entrance. "Relax." I relax my muscles, which I didn't even realize were tensing up.

His thumb strokes my clit, and I grip his shoulder and dig my nails in. "Oh god," I moan at the feeling of being stretched.

Little by little, he makes his way inside me. He pulls out and moves back in with little strokes, to get me adjusted.

Once he is finally all the way inside me, our eyes connect. "You're so beautiful, my Gracelyn." He kisses me, just as he moves slowly inside me. He takes my hands and presses them above my head, our fingers entwined.

With every movement, every single touch, I feel so cherished. He makes sure I'm okay, and this is one of the best moments of my life.

This is a big deal to me.

I wrap my arms around his neck, holding on, as I get closer and closer to the edge, my breathing becoming more rapid.

"Harder," I plead. I'm right there but I need more.

He moves faster, harder, and with each stroke he grinds against my clit. I bite his shoulder, my whole body shaking, and then I explode.

I go limp as I convulse around him. He continues to move inside me to prolong the orgasm before I feel him explode.

He groans deeply in my ear. I love that I gave him that much pleasure. I run my hands down his back as we both come down from the high.

He slowly slides out of me, and we lie together trying to catch our breaths. I press kisses against his cheek, head, and shoulder, loving every second of this.

"I will be back."

He walks into the bathroom, and I grin and stare at the ceiling. I'm really happy. I've thought so many times that I would never be happy. I felt like I was cursed, but I now know that the perfect man was made for me—he just had to come into my life.

He walks out of the bathroom holding a washcloth. "What are..." I stop as he presses the warm cloth between my legs, cleaning me.

He looks at me. "What?"

I probably have a crazy look on my face; I am trying my best not to cry because that was so sweet.

"You're just perfect," I tell him honestly.

He tugs on my toe. "No, that's you, sweetheart." He tosses the washcloth into the bathroom and climbs in bed with me. He pulls me against him until my head is resting on his chest. I think I could do this every single night for the rest of my life.

He slowly drags his fingers across my back. "Sleep, baby."

I close my eyes and I fall asleep in seconds.

Aiden

Today has been a long day, but it ended on the best note it could have. I knew she needed this—and I loved every second of it—but it hurt me knowing that she was so scared. Seeing the fear on her face will forever haunt me.

The second she let that go, she changed right before my eyes.

I am so fucking honored that she let me be the one to help her let go.

It fucking kills me knowing her father is out there right now, breathing. He doesn't deserve a single second after what he did.

I am in awe of how strong she is. She has been so brave and unbelievably strong, doing it all alone.

I hold her a little tighter. I don't sleep for hours, listening to the sound of her breathing.

9

GRACE

AIDEN AND I WALK HAND IN HAND TO THE BACK OF THE CLUBHOUSE, where everyone is grilling and hanging out. Aiden is carrying Reid.

I spot Amelia standing next to Lane, helping him with the food. I also see a lot of people I don't know. They are wearing cuts for a different club: Devil Souls MC.

Travis walks out of the clubhouse with Aiden, and Bailey walks over to me. "Want a drink? We have some daiquiris if you want one."

I usually don't drink, but I think one won't hurt. "Sure." I slip my hand from Aiden's. "I will be back."

Amelia joins us, and a bunch of other girls come from the group of Devils Souls guys. I look back and smile at all of them, and they return it. In the kitchen I lean against the counter looking at the newcomers.

Amelia points to the first girl, who looks a lot like Lane and Smiley. "This is Shaylin. She is Lane's sister."

She points to the girl next to her. "This is Kayla. She is the VP's ole lady." She is beautiful, and her hair is to die for.

Next to her is a girl who, for some reason, I see a lot of myself in. I can tell, right off the bat, she has fought some demons. "This is Alisha, Techy's ole lady. She is Adeline's daughter—Adeline is Smiley's Ole Lady."

The next girl appears to be the youngest. "This is Paisley. She is Torch and Kayla's daughter and Liam's ole lady."

"It's nice to meet all of you." I smile warmly.

I can tell these ladies are just as nice as the Grim Sinners girls. "I don't know about you girls, but I think a girls' night needs to happen," Kayla tells all of us.

"Yes! I would love that."

We all make small talk and make plans for the following weekend. When we return to the party, Aiden is sitting in a chair, holding a beer, talking to a few guys I don't know. I walk over and sit in his lap.

"This is Gracie, this is Torch and Techy. They are members of the Devils."

"It's nice to meet you guys. I was just talking to your ladies. We have plans, next weekend, for a girls' night."

Both of them pale and I look at Aiden, who is just grinning. They excuse themselves. "Did I say something wrong?"

"Oh no, the girls tend to get into trouble if they're all together."

"Ahh, that makes sense. You don't care?" I pull his arm into my lap.

"Nah, I trust my girl." He nips the side of my neck, causing me to laugh. I settle back into his arms, enjoying being around good company and spending time with Aiden. Reid is being passed around to all the ole ladies.

Aiden's mom walks in at the exact moment Walker steps out of the clubhouse. He looks around and his eyes land on her. He stares at her before a slow grin comes over his face, and he walks over to her.

Uhh oh.

"What the fuck?" Aiden snarls and I try not to laugh. I think Walker would be so good for Laurie. She deserves to be happy.

Walker takes her dish from her, and she laughs at something he says. Together they take the plate to the table.

"What is he doing with my mother?" Aiden looks so traumatized.

"Honey, your mom is gorgeous and Walker is single."

His eyes widen as the dots connect. "Not my mother." His voice is higher and I cover my face laughing. It makes me wonder how he would be if he had a daughter and she tried to date. "Baby." I laugh and hug him; he is being so cute.

Amelia walks over to us with Reid in her arms. "I think someone is missing his parents."

My heart skips a beat at her calling me his parent. I love the sound of that.

Tiffany sits down in the chair next to me and Aiden. "How are you enjoying your week off from practice?" I ask her. Since we don't have any games coming up anytime soon, I let them have the time off.

"I love practice, so not so much," she confesses and I laugh.

"I was the same way when I played."

She looks off for a second, and I can tell she wants to say something. "Leah came to school today with a bruise on her neck. She could barely talk."

I close my eyes. "I will do something about it, honey." I touch her hand and she nods, looking sad.

Leah lives with her mother and stepfather, and I know both of them are on drugs. When I saw the bruises, I asked the person who owns the center if he knew anything about her case. Apparently, social workers had been called in the past, but nothing has happened. It looks like I'm going to be calling the social workers again. My heart hurts for her, and it hits a bit too close to home for me.

Tiffany sits higher in her seat. "Let's have a softball game, us against the guys."

"Let's do it." I slide out of Aiden's lap. "Do you have a bat and ball?"

She gives me a look that says *duh*. "Of course I do." She runs to her dad, and I know she is telling him her idea.

"You ready to get your butt whooped?" I wink at Aiden.

He smirks. "Baby, the only thing getting whooped is your ass later."

I feel my face heat, and I peek around to make sure no one heard what he just said. "Your daddy is just crazy." I rock Reid side to side, enjoying snuggling with him.

A few minutes later Tiffany walks out of the clubhouse carrying a couple of balls and her bat.

"I'm going to take Reid to your mom," I tell Aiden.

His mother is still talking to Walker. I sneak over. "Do you mind watching him while we play softball?" I ask her.

I caught the tail end of their conversation. Walker was asking about tomorrow night. Do they have a date? Aiden will be pissed, but I am excited for her.

"Sure, honey." She takes Reid from me, and I leave her to finish their convo.

We all file out into the field behind the clubhouse. Tiffany is already standing on the pitcher's mound. I take my hair tie off my wrist, put my hair in a bun, and head to first base.

"Have any of you guys played before?" I ask Amelia, Shaylin, Joslyn, Bailey, Paisley, and Alisha.

Shaylin, Amelia, Paisley, and Bailey raise their hands. "Okay you guys, hit the bases." The others hit the outfields. We all slip on our gloves. Tiffany has a shit ton of gear; she brings extra gear to practice for others who need it.

One by one the guys make their way over to us, with all of their swagger. They think they've got it in the bag. Tiffany winks at me, and I hold back my laughter. Don't underestimate me or Tiffany.

Tiffany's face lights up when Travis steps up to bat. I know this means a lot to her. This would have been my dream when I was her age.

Travis raises his bat but his form, in holding the bat, is completely off. I know one thing: Tiffany is not going to hold back against Travis the way she usually does when pitching to other girls.

Not my girls though. I've trained them hard to be the best, and when they're older, I want them all to get scholarships so they can be whatever they want to be in life.

Tiffany nods and then throws. Lane is standing behind Travis, being the catcher. I guess he is going to be the umpire.

"Strike."

Travis looks slightly rattled. I grin. Tiffany pretends not to be affected. She throws again, harder. "Strike!" Lane calls again. Tiffany pushes her ponytail over her shoulder, pulling her cap down over her eyes.

She relaxes her stance, and I know she is going to let him hit the ball. She throws a slower pitch, and he hits it. Amelia picks up the ball and throws it. I run to the right to catch it, because she threw wide.

"Out!"

I throw the ball to Tiffany, and she kicks the dirt as Aiden comes up to bat. He lifts the bat, and I know immediately that he's played before.

Tiffany looks at me and I nod, letting her know to go full force. She throws and he hits it to the outfield. Joslyn runs and swipes it off the ground; it goes to Paisley and then to me. I jump, catching it in the air, and touch Aiden just as he reaches me.

"Hot fucking damn. I see why she's Tiffany's coach," Travis says from the back of the line.

"Grace, let's change out," Tiffany says and I grin. Wilder is up next, and I know he's played baseball, because Aiden has mentioned it.

I walk over and take Tiffany's place. I nod and Wilder readies his stance. I throw the ball as you would in baseball. Wilder's eyes widen as the ball hits Lane's mitt. "Strike!"

"That's my girl!" Aiden calls and I shake my head, laughing at his goofiness. Wilder schools his face, and I know he isn't playing anymore.

I throw and he hits it. It slides right down by my foot, and I kneel to catch it. I throw it to Tiffany, who catches it. I blow on my hand and dust off my shoulders; I may be a bit cocky. I put the ball down, and now it's our turn to hit.

Tiffany is full-out laughing as she runs to my side. "They never expected that," she gloats. "We showed them." I raise my hand and she smacks it.

I am first in line. I take the bat and twirl it around in my hand a second before settling into my stance. The pitcher is Torch from the Devils Souls; Lane is still the catcher. He got the gear from Tiffany.

Torch throws the ball, and I don't try to hit it the first time. I like to get a feel for their pitches before I swing.

I take a deep breath and let it out slowly, and Torch pitches. Whack! My bat hits the ball, letting it soar to the outfield.

My bat hits the ground, and I take off in a sprint. I make it to second base right before Liam, Paisley's husband, catches up to me.

Tiffany is up next and I move a bit off base, ready. Torch throws the ball, and Tiffany hits it on the first pitch. I take off running, making it to third, and Tiffany gets to first.

Paisley is up next. She moves into her stance and Torch pitches. She nicks it and I still take off sprinting. I slide into home and Tiffany moves to third as they get Paisley out.

The game continues for a while, and we have four home runs

before we call it quits. The guys accept the loss, and Tiffany is eating up the fact she beat all of these bikers.

Aiden makes his way to my side and taps me slightly on the ass. "You're beautiful."

I move up on my tippy toes and kiss him. "Thank you, baby." I run my hands down his arms.

We make our way back to the clubhouse, where the food is ready. I take Reid back from Laurie, and Aiden carries our food to a table. After we sit down, Laurie joins us, with Walker right beside her.

"Bastard," Aiden grumbles under his breath, and it takes everything in me not to burst out laughing.

"Aiden, can you hand me his blanket? It's getting kind of chilly." The sun is starting to go down, and the temperature is dropping. I cover up his little legs and lay my head on Aiden's shoulder for a second before I go back to eating.

Everything happens in slow motion. I hear the screech of a vehicle, and I look over just as someone rolls down a window. A guy steps out and I scream, wanting everyone to get out of the way. I am picked up off my chair and set on the ground. Aiden tosses the table over, and I lie on the ground, holding Reid under my body.

Aiden puts his body over both of us, and Walker lies on top of Laurie, right beside us, as they open fire.

It feels like it goes on forever. Then it stops and starts up again, but the sound of the gun firing is much closer. I peek over and see Lucas and a few others returning fire.

Then the vehicle zooms away, and Aiden slowly moves aside. I sit up and clutch Reid to my body. I am shaking with terror.

"Baby, get inside. We are going after them," Aiden tells me. I take Laurie's hand, and the rest of the ladies and kids rush into the clubhouse.

I look at the surveillance screen on the wall. All the guys are leaving and rushing after the shooters.

I settle onto the couch, trying to catch my breath. Some of the other ladies are doing the same thing. I never expected for that to happen.

Aiden covered my body; he would have taken a bullet for me and Reid. Everyone's first priority was the women and kids.

Amelia sits down beside me, with Tiffany at her feet, and I can tell that she is scared. Hell, we all are. We were eating our food and enjoying ourselves—then bam!

Luckily, no one was hurt. That would have been devastating.

Aiden

I can't fucking believe someone openly attacked us right on the grounds of the clubhouse, with the women and children.

You can fuck with us, but when you come for the ones we care about most, then this is a whole different fucking kind of war. You're asking to be left in pieces; you're asking to be fucking destroyed. That's one thing this club and the Devils don't tolerate: when their families are in danger.

We are close on the van's ass, and Logan is shooting at it. The van stops all of a sudden; Logan must have hit one of their front tires. We rush the van and rip them out of it. They start screaming and pleading immediately.

One of them screams, "We didn't hurt anyone!" He's holding his face, trying to curl himself into a ball as best he can, like that can protect him. No, that protection left the second he raised a gun to my family. The fucking thought of one of those bullets hitting Grace, Reid, or my mother...

"Shut the fuck up." I grab the back of his neck and drop him so he face plants onto the ground.

One of our vans pulls up, and a couple of prospects jump out and push them into the back of the vehicle. "To the back of the property," Lane tells the prospects.

We recently constructed a new building, on the back of our

property, for things like this. We want to make sure the women and children in the club aren't exposed to any of that.

Walker is standing a few feet away from me, and I walk over. "I want to thank you for protecting my mother."

"It wasn't nothing, brother." He stops and gives me a look that makes me think I am not going to like what he's about to to say. "I am taking your mother out on a date tomorrow night."

Yeah, I knew I wasn't going to like it, but she is a grown woman and Walker isn't a bad guy. I know he will take care of her.

I grind my jaw a second before I nod. "Be good to her or else." I don't give a fuck if he is my brother or not.

"Don't worry about that." He winks and my stomach churns. I hope the fuck he doesn't mean what I think he does.

I climb back on my bike and follow the others back to the building, where we will extract information the hard way if necessary.

The prospects walk them over to the chains hanging from the ceiling. We do this because it's more painful than sitting and it's harder to escape.

Lane and Kyle are front and center, facing them dead on. I would not want to fucking be them now.

The door opens, revealing Liam. Yeah, I wouldn't want to fucking be them, because Liam is a badass who was trained in this shit.

"This can go two ways. You can tell us and you die, or we can force it out of you and you die." Lane leans forward, in one guy's face. "Very painfully."

The guy starts shaking, and sweat pours off his face. I can smell him from here, and I'm halfway across the room. I can tell that he is on drugs on top of all that. The other guy is silent. I can tell that he has a bit more willpower. But this guy looks like he's about to cry."

"Man, I don't want to die. I was just doing what I was paid to do." He breaks down sobbing.

Shit, already?

I know we're probably scary to those who have wronged us, but it's also kind of fucking pathetic. *You had enough balls to shoot at a courtyard full of motorcycle club members, filled with women and kids.*

That is unforgivable. They're not leaving here, but we will have mercy if they tell us what's needed.

"Who paid you?" Kyle walks closer, which I wouldn't recommend because it's rank.

The sweaty dude looks at the guy next to him, who still hasn't said a word. "Fuck!" he screams. "It was the head guy of the trafficking ring you've been taking down little by little. He is getting desperate."

Well, I guess that answers that. The guys look around at each other. I think we all suspected it was related to the trafficking. It's serious shit. People like that are the worst of the worst, and we've almost completely torn their business apart. They don't want that, but it's not going to happen in our backyard. My son was a victim of that ring, and I know I won't rest until it's destroyed.

I hear two gunshots. Kyle and Lane just shot both of them, killing them instantly.

Lane turns to look at all of us. "Let's get back to our women and children. Tomorrow we will discuss this and come up with a plan of action."

I am one of the first ones out the door. I want to make sure my family is okay. Grace was terrified; I could see it all over her face. Hell, all the old ladies were. If the gate had been shut, the bullets wouldn't have made it through. But this was an open event.

In the clubhouse, Gracelyn is on the couch, next to my mom, holding Reid. Fuck, she looks exhausted.

I bend down in front of her. "Ready to go home, baby?" I push her hair out of her face.

She touches my hand; then she holds it, closing her eyes. "Yeah, take me home." I help her off the couch. She's still holding my son, who is chewing on a teething ring.

"Mom, want me to take you home?"

"I can take her." Walker pops out of nowhere, taking my mom's keys out of her hand, and I want to tell him to leave her the fuck alone.

"Yeah baby, take me home." She slides off the couch and stands beside Walker. I guess that is that. Grace tries to hide her smile.

She gets way too much enjoyment out of my frustration.

I take Reid from her. "Come on." I kiss the side of her head and lead her to the truck. The gate is shut at the moment, so the courtyard will be safe.

Grace

This has probably been one of the scariest days of my life. I was terrified of someone getting hurt, and then I was terrified when Aiden went after them.

I sat on that couch with Laurie, and all the women were silent, waiting for their family to come back safe. It was so heroic how the first instinct of every single member of the club was to protect. These men are a different breed for sure.

We are driving off; it's getting late and I know Reid has to be exhausted. I know I am.

I unbuckle myself and scoot into the middle, and I lay my head on Aiden's shoulder. I need to feel him right now; he makes me feel so safe.

"You okay?" he asks.

"I'm fine, trust me." I kiss his arm and close my eyes, breathing his scent in deeply. And I am. With Aiden, everything just seems better.

10

GRACE

TODAY IS ONE THAT I'M NOT LOOKING FORWARD TO ONE BIT. TODAY is the day they're burying my aunt.

I don't want to go, because so many people will be there that I just can't stand. Vomit crawls up my throat at the thought of seeing my father and uncle. I press my hands against the counter, trying to brace myself for what's to come and calm my nerves.

Arms wrap around my waist. I open my eyes and, in the mirror, my and Aiden's eyes connect.

"It will be fine, sweet girl."

I look away; I don't want to be upset. I know it's going to be fine, but bringing up old memories doesn't sound fun at the moment. Mainly because I am in a very good place. I did a lot of healing before I met Aiden, and got over many of my fears with his help. I don't want anything to set me back, but I also know they have only as much power over me as I allow.

Aiden turns me around. "Baby."

I look up.

"You're safe with me. No matter what, I will be there for you, and if you want I will kick their asses out."

I smile tearfully, and I move closer and just hug him. His arms encircle me, and I bask in the moment of peace.

Is it too soon to say that every second I am in his arms is one of complete, utter peace? It's like I'm finally home, and I know where I'm meant to be in life.

"Let's do this," I tell him. I put on my big-girl panties, and I am going to face this head-on.

I am not the same girl, and it's time to prove that to them.

BEFORE WE GET to the funeral home, I hear a ton of bikes pulling up behind us. I am shocked to see all the members of the Grim Sinners behind us.

As we pull in front of the home, I can see the strange looks we're getting. Aiden turns off the bike. "What are you guys doing here?" I ask Amelia.

She wraps her arm around me. "Do you think we're going to let you go to war without us? You're ours and we have your back."

Tears fill my eyes at the sight of everyone being here to support me. They are the best. "Thank you guys so much." I hug Amelia, and she pats my back. "You're family, it's what we're here for."

For the first time in my life, I know what family is. No one has ever cared enough to make sure I'm okay. I can't tell you one nice thing anyone did for me before I met Aiden. He has completely flipped my life upside down.

The whole MC has.

Aiden takes my hand, and we lead the group inside the home. We pass a few of my distant family members gawking at the door.

Aunt Mary's husband, my uncle, is in the front pew. He is one of the men I hate more than anything in the world. And my father is beside him. He is staring at me. This is a different look than the one I saw at the hospital. This is one of pure anger.

I clear my throat, straighten my shoulders, and walk to the casket, feeling the eyes of others staring a hole in my back. I haven't seen these people since I was eleven years old. I step up to the casket and, from the corner of my eye, I see my sperm donor stepping forward like he is going to do something about it. In a split second, Aiden is between us.

I pay my respects and take my seat with the rest of the MC. They take up a lot of rows of seats.

"I'm going to go to the bathroom." I kiss Aiden's cheek and try to sneak off to the bathroom before the service starts. I try to ignore the looks of everyone I walk past. I am, apparently, the person who tried to ruin the whole family.

I told the police everything. I was terrified but I wanted it all to end. I would rather be in foster care than live through another second of that abuse.

I never expected my mother's parents to take me in, and I am eternally grateful. It was the first home I'd ever had—maybe not the most welcoming, but it was heaven compared to what I was used to.

I remember the first night I went to sleep without fearing for my life. I'd always walked on eggshells, and now I didn't have to. It took a long time to adjust to not waiting for the ball to drop.

I wash my hands; I needed this second alone to gather my thoughts. The door opens and Aunt Glenna steps inside the bathroom. I look at her face in shock. Someone beat the shit out of her. The door slams shut, and I fold my arms across my chest, bracing myself.

She glares at me, and I arch an eyebrow. Does she think that I am going to be scared of her?

"Look what the fuck you did to my face," she screeches and starts toward me, her hands stretched out.

The door opens, and Aiden walks inside and grabs her by the hair before she can reach me. "I know you weren't about to fucking touch my woman."

The others file into the bathroom, with Amelia right in the front. "Are you asking to get your ass kicked again?" *Again?* I look at the group in front of me confused.

Aiden pushes her toward Shaylin, who smacks her hard across the face. He puts his hands on my shoulders. "Baby, I know you're wondering why. They hurt you, and they needed to pay for that shit."

I close my eyes and rest my head on his chest, breathing in deeply, letting his words sink in. I have no regrets. "How many were involved in this?" I ask.

"The whole club," he says. I look over at the others. They're willing to go to these lengths to protect me and get justice, and right now they have my back.

"Thank you guys so much."

Amelia grips Glenna's throat hard, and my aunt latches onto her hand, trying to pull her loose. "I will let you fucking live because this is a funeral," Amelia says. "If you try that shit again, it will be the end of you."

Lane is behind her, smirking, all too proud of her being all badass. "Ready to get back out there?" Lane asks me.

I nod. "Yeah, let's do this." I follow the group back to our seats. My father is sitting just a few feet from me. On one side of me is Aiden, and Amelia is on the other.

The service is probably ten minutes max. No one speaks besides the pastor. Her entire life in a ten-minute service. It makes me so sad that she lived this life and never got to experience happiness.

Meanwhile her husband is laughing and having the time of his life. He spent his whole life with her and he's laughing.

Once the service is over, I walk over to her casket. "Rest easy, Mary. You're free now."

I take peace in knowing she's not in hell anymore.

Aiden

Her fucking aunt tried to attack her. Apparently, she has shit for brains.

Gracelyn is standing at the casket saying her final goodbye. I look around and see so many fucking eyes on us; none of these people are good. I can look at them and tell they're mean.

They hate her; I can feel that shit. I know my brothers feel it, and I know Gracelyn knows.

Nobody spoke to her. They just looked at her like she was gum at the bottom of their shoe.

I looked at the police report after Gracelyn told me about her home life. She exposed her family's drug abuse. That affected the whole family; it shut them down and a lot of them went to jail. They placed all the blame on an eleven-year-old girl who was just trying to protect herself.

I rub her arm as she says her final goodbyes. She looks at me sadly, but I can tell that she feels better in a way. "Ready to go?" I ask.

She nods, pushing a piece of her hair behind her ear. "I need to get out of here."

We walk toward the doors, and the MC follows us. Our bikes are parked up front. I sigh with relief.

Grace

The door slams open, and my father, uncle, and a bunch of my cousins come out.

Please tell me this isn't what I think it is.

I grab Aiden's hand tightly. Why are they doing this? Why can't they just let me leave?

"Do you fucking think you guys can come in here and act like you own it? I don't think so," my father yells, causing me to flinch.

Amelia walks over to me and holds my hand, and Aiden steps in front of both of us. "You need to shut your mouth and walk back inside or you're going to regret it," Aiden snarls in a voice I have never heard from him.

I grip the back of his shirt, unable to stop shaking. I'm not exactly scared, but me and confrontation don't mix. I peek around his arm and see my father is way closer than I thought. I decide to do something about it.

I step out and stand next to Aiden. "Don't forget, I can put you away again."

My father takes a step back. I said enough to lock them away before, but I didn't reveal everything.

One by one they leave, and I want to fall to the ground and sleep the day away. When I get overwhelmed, I just want to sleep and forget what happened.

"Baby, what do you have over them?" he asks, as I look at their retreating backs.

"They have a place outside of town where they make meth, and they sell it throughout Texas."

Aiden looks at Lane and I see him nod. "Do you want to do something about it?" Lane asks.

Do I want to end it? They shouldn't be able to continue to do horrible things. So many people suffer because of these drugs.

"I think they need to be stopped. They've gotten away with so much." I have seen people overdose right before my eyes. They used to force people to take the drugs to make sure they were correctly made. Sometimes it wasn't and people died.

I feel eyes on me, and I see my uncle standing by his car. He rubs his dick in a gross gesture. I cover my mouth so don't puke.

"I fucking saw that," Bailey hisses and points in his direction.

Aiden starts to run over, but I grab the back of his pants and Lane pushes his chest. "This is not the place, Aiden. It will all come to pass soon," Lane promises him.

I rub Aiden's back, trying to calm him. He is shaking hard with his fists clenched. I tug him so he turns around, and I place my hands on his face. "Baby, let's go see Reid—yeah?" I try to lead him away.

Little by little, his breathing returns to normal. "There's my Aidey," I tease and he laughs.

"Thank you so much, everyone, for being here today." I put my hand over my heart. I love everyone here.

"It's what family is for," Joslyn pipes in and I smile.

"Yeah," I whisper. I am getting that for the first time.

No more being alone.

11

GRACE

A week later

I AM IN THE BACKYARD, PLAYING WITH REID IN HIS SANDBOX. IT'S A beautiful day. Aiden will be home from running errands any minute.

The funeral service brought us even closer. Little by little, my walls are breaking down around him. I started telling him more of my past; he genuinely wants to know everything about me. It's difficult to bring up all these memories I have shut down, but it's so freeing at the same time.

Day by day, I am healing more and more. I have always done it all alone but now, with Aiden, I am seeing things differently. I thought no one could accept my past but, in the end, I was wrong.

A song comes over the radio, and Aiden bends down and picks me up off the ground. I kiss him as he dances with me. My heart is just filled with so much love. Every single day he surprises me with something. One of the things I love most about him is how he is with Reid. He is so hands-on with everything.

"Da!" Reid is staring at both of us.

Aiden sets me down and lifts him up, cuddling him. "I missed you, my boy." My heart warms at the sight of them together.

"I wonder how your mom's date went the other day," I ask, knowing very well I'm throwing gasoline on the fire.

He glares at me in mock anger. "Don't start that shit."

I laugh, smacking him hard on the ass. "Or what are you going to do about it?" I run inside the house to hide.

I head upstairs, into one of the guest rooms and into the bathroom, and I climb under the kitchen sink. His footsteps are loud against the hardwood floor—oh wait. I hid a water gun in here. I grab it and fill it as fast as I can. Then I slide back under the counter, holding my water pistol, giggling to myself. My heart is pounding as he gets closer and closer.

I hold my breath when I hear him outside the bathroom door. I position myself as quietly as possible so when he opens the door I can spray.

He opens the cabinet doors and I spray him. He jumps back and I crawl out. He wraps his hands around my feet, and I snort with laughter as he drags me toward him. I flip over onto my back as he grabs my arms, pinning them above my head. He nibbles the side of my neck.

I tilt my head to the side. "Where's Reid?" I ask, my voice already breathless.

"He is in his playpen," he says between kisses, licks, and bites. He grips the bottom of my shirt and pulls it above my head. He buries his head between my breasts and blows. I laugh and twist to the side. He pins my arms above my head again and moves further down, biting my sides.

"Uncle!" I scream with laughter, tears rolling down my face.

He pulls away, laughing; then he stands, taking me with him. He carries me to the bed and throws me down. I bounce and he pulls my shorts off.

I smirk at the sight of his face when he realizes I'm not

wearing underwear. He runs his finger along the insides of my thighs. "Was my baby thinking she was going to get some?"

I lick my lips, and his eyes darken. I love the effect that I have on him. I have never felt so beautiful and empowered.

"I didn't mean to be cocky, but...." I look at his dick, making my point known, and he is rock hard.

He smirks, knowing he is caught, and he gets down on his knees. He wraps his arms around my legs and pulls me until I am practically seated on his face. He licks me from top to bottom, and my legs shake instantly. He eats me like a man starved.

Right when I'm about to come, he pulls away. "You're going to come on my dick." He pulls his pants down and I crawl up the bed, making sure my ass sways, teasing him.

He kisses my stomach and moves between my thighs, and I circle my legs around him. My eyes roll back in my head when he slowly slides inside me. I'm already close from the almost-orgasm I just had.

I open my eyes and look at Aiden, who is staring down at me with so much tenderness and love.

Love.

I cup the sides of his face, pushing the small strands of hair aside. "I love you, so much." One part of me is utterly terrified of what he will say, but I feel so safe with him I can tell him anything.

His head falls until our foreheads are touching. "I love you too, my Grace," he whispers back. In that second, a part of me I never knew was missing is finally in place. I know he is the one for me. The one I'm going to spend the rest of my life with.

I feel this to my very soul.

This is one of the most magical moments of my life, being connected to someone on this level. This is what I have always dreamed of, but it's better because I'm living it. So much better than I thought it would ever be.

A couple of months ago, I never would have thought this

could happen. Then he popped into my life, and it changed in a split second.

I have not been back home in days. I go home to get clothes, and then I come right back here.

Later, he picks me up off the guest bed, carries me into our room, and lays me down on the bed. "Sleep, baby. I will fix dinner." I pull the blanket over me and fall asleep almost instantly.

∾

MY PHONE STARTS RINGING. I look over at the clock and see it's eleven. The call is from Leah. She is calling from the phone I bought her, which she occasionally uses to text me to see if there's practice.

"Hello?"

I hear crying. "Mrs. Gracie."

I sit up in bed, already terrified at the sound of her voice. I can tell something is seriously wrong.

"What's wrong?" I ask her, putting it on speakerphone so Aiden can hear too.

"My stepdad is being meaner than usual. I'm really scared," she whispers into the phone.

Aiden has his phone out, texting someone.

"What's happening, honey?" I get up, leaving the phone on the bed so I can talk to her as I get dressed.

"He is really high on drugs, he hit me bad this time. I'm scared. He is in the living room throwing things. My mom hasn't been home for days, and I'm really hungry." Her voice is shaking.

I look at Aiden in panic when I hear loud pounding on her door. "Let me in!" I hear a man yell. I cover my mouth, terrified for her. I'm not there and there's nothing I can do. Aiden is putting on his jeans and grabbing his guns.

"I will be there asap, sweetheart," I tell her, and I run downstairs and put my shoes on.

"Aiden, is someone coming to be with Reid?" I ask, my heart racing. I can still hear Leah's stepfather screaming in the background.

"Joslyn is walking over right now."

I walk outside with Aiden, and Joslyn is walking up the drive. "Thank you so much," I say.

"No thanks needed." Joslyn is carrying her toddler on her hip.

Wilder, Lane, and Logan pull up on their bikes, and Aiden starts his truck. I hurry into the truck, and we roar out of the gated community. I tell him her address; it's in a very bad part of town. "We are a few minutes away, honey," I tell Leah, listening to her stepdad pounding on her door.

"Okay." She's so quiet.

I close my eyes at this horrible situation; it's one that I can relate to. You're so terrified that you're afraid to breathe in case they hear you or you trigger them.

It's literal hell being so scared all the time.

A few minutes later we pull up in front of the most horrendous house. It looks like it's going to fall down any second. The middle of the roof is sunken in; with one huge wind, I know it would collapse.

I get out and Aiden walks over to me. "Stay right by my side, baby." Yeah, there's no way I will be out of his sight.

Lane, Wilder, and Logan stand next to us. Wilder runs to the back of the house, and I stand behind the guys as they walk up to the porch.

Aiden kicks and the door falls in, and I hurry up the steps, following them into the house. The first thing that hits me is the heat. The house is really hot, and the smell is just as bad.

I look around the living room. There's a leather couch that I suppose was white at one point, but it's covered in mold. The walls are covered in black mold, and the floor is full of holes. One wrong step could have you falling through.

I hear Leah's stepfather screaming as he runs into the living room to see what all the commotion is. Aiden moves forward and grabs him by the throat. I sneak past and run down the hallway to Leah.

"Leah? It's me." I call, knocking gently on the locked door.

Slowly the door opens a crack and she opens it. I take in the sight of her face, and fury like I have ever felt before in my life hits me.

Her face...

Her eyes are black and her cheekbone is bruised. "Oh, sweetheart." I hug her and she cries into my shoulder.

I know one thing: I will make sure she never has to experience this again. "Go pack your bag."

Her eyes light up with hope before she drops her head. "Where will I go?"

"Do you have any other family?" I push her hair out of her face.

She shakes her head. "My mom was a foster kid, she never had a family, and I don't know my dad."

My heart breaks for this little girl. She is truly alone in this world, and I don't want to know what she has suffered. "You will come with me." I will do whatever it takes for her to come live with me if it's what she wants.

She hurries into her room to pack her bag, and I shut her door gently. I am shaking from head to toe, I am so mad. Who does he think he is, hitting a little girl?

I notice her softball bat leaning against the couch in the living room, and I snatch it up and walk over to her stepfather with one thing on my mind.

To beat his ass.

Aiden sees me coming, and his eyes widen as he sees my expression. I am someone who rarely gets mad.

This is unforgivable.

"You should see her face." I shake my head, wanting the image out of my mind forever.

"Yeah, what the fuck you going to do about it?" Leah's stepfather says.

"You're just a pathetic piece of shit, do you know that? You're weak and you have to beat babies to feel like something." I grab my bat and swing, hitting him across the knee.

He starts to scream, but Logan covers his mouth so Leah doesn't hear. I smack him hard across the face. "It doesn't feel good to be hit, does it?"

He shakes his head. He can't stand on the leg I hit with the bat. I hope I busted it.

"Where is her mother?" I ask. I need to make sure her mother isn't coming back.

He laughs. "That bitch left. She packed her stuff and left with some guy to go to California."

I just don't understand how parents can be so heartless. Now that Reid is a part of my life, I could never imagine just leaving.

I look at Aiden. "I want her to come live with me, she has no one," I whisper, not wanting her to hear.

He corrects me. "Come live with *us.*"

I smile. I hoped he would say something like that. "With us." I say.

I hear footsteps coming down the hall, and Leah walks into the living room. *Her face.* I close my eyes a second, trying not to beat the shit out of him in front of her.

I hear growls all around me. I look at the guys, and I know they're seconds away from killing him.

"Sweetheart, are you sure you want to come live with me?" I ask her one last time.

"And me," Aiden pipes in.

"I am sure." She looks at her stepdad, terrified.

"I will have the paperwork to you by morning. It pays to have people in your pocket." Lane winks. I love that I won't have to deal with the courts, and we can get all of this settled as soon as possible.

I walk to the door, my hand outstretched. "Come on, sweetheart, let's get your stuff in the truck." She walks over to me without looking at her stepdad.

One thing is for sure: I am going to give her whatever she needs. Therapy is going to be a priority. If I had started it when I was younger, I think my life would have been better. I waited until I was older, and destructive ideas were stuck in my head, so it was hard for me to change my way of thinking about certain things.

I look over my shoulder and nod at the stepdad. This is my way of giving Aiden permission to beat his ass. Aiden smirks at me like I'm hilarious for thinking anything different. I shut the door behind me, and I open the back seat for Leah to get inside. I get in the front, and I turn around in my seat so I can look at her. She is staring out the window like the world is on her shoulders.

Her mother just up and left her with someone who abused her. Honestly, this life is all she has known, and now she is going somewhere different.

It's scary.

"It's going to be okay. I know how you feel," I tell her softly, my heart breaking a little when her tear-filled eyes meet mine.

"How?" she asks.

"I was in a very similar situation when I was your age. It's scary but your life is going to be different now. I will take care of you, and you will never have to worry again." I don't know what else to say.

She sniffs, her tears falling, and I gently wipe them away. I wish I could just take the pain from her.

"Like I'm your daughter?" she asks.

I smile. "Yes, if you want to be."

She smiles for the first time, giving me a glimpse of the little girl I have come to love. "Yes, I would."

That just made my day, my year. "I would love that," I tell her honestly. This little girl has been on my mind every single day since I met her. I know, in this moment, she was meant to be mine. I was meant to take her out of this situation and give her the life she deserves. Her life is going to be different from mine. I am going to make sure she thrives and all this shit doesn't affect her like it did me.

A few minutes later Aiden walks out with the guys. I can tell by the satisfied look on his face he beat some ass.

I can't believe that I slapped Leah's stepfather and took out his knee. That is so out of character for me. I was just so mad. I know this happens, but seeing it happen to her hit really close to home, and I wanted to let him know that what he did is wrong.

"Myra is on her way to the house so we can get her checked out."

"That makes me feel better."

I peek back at Leah. She watches her house until it's out of sight. I hate that she has to do this but, honestly, that house wasn't fit for her to live in.

"So, Leah, Tiffany and I beat the guys in the MC at softball. I think a rematch is in order, with you showing them what you can do." I look back and wink at her.

She giggles. "That's right, Miss Gracie."

"Just call me Grace or whatever you want, okay?" I don't want her to feel obligated to call me Miss Gracie anymore.

"Okay." She holds her bag in her lap.

I turn around and let the tears fall, and Aiden and Leah are silent as I stare ahead. Aiden touches my face, and I look over.

"It will be fine," he mouths to me.

I nod and wipe my tears off my face, and I let out a deep breath. I need to be strong for her.

We reach the community, the gate opens, and we pull into our drive. One thing I love about this is that everyone lives close together. The first part of the community is like a suburb. Farther down there's a tract of land accommodating bigger houses, and you have the option to build your own. It's really safe. The kids can play outside and do whatever they want without the fear of something happening, because only MC members live here.

"This is your house?" She sits forward, her eyes wide.

"Your house now," Aiden tells her, and I fall a bit more in love with him.

I get out and open her door. I take her bag from her and lead her up the steps. A strange vehicle is already here, and my guess is it's the doctor.

Aiden walks in first, with me and Leah behind him. Joslyn is in the living room with another woman, who I assume is Myra.

"Hi, this must be Leah." Myra gets off the couch and Joslyn follows suit.

"Thank you so much for babysitting for us." I hug Joslyn and she waves her arm. "No big deal."

I turn my attention to Leah, who is nervous; she is chewing on her nails.

"I'm a doctor," Myra says. "I want to check to make sure you're okay."

I hand Aiden Leah's bag, and I follow them into the kitchen, where Myra has Leah sit on a barstool at the island. "I need you to tell me where you hurt, okay?" Myra tells her.

Leah looks at me. "It's okay, sweetheart," I tell her.

She points to her face; then she lifts her shirt and I can see bruises on her stomach. "My head is sore, he dragged me by my hair."

I close my eyes at the realization of how horrible her life has been. I should have done something sooner, and I will forever have that regret resting on my shoulders.

Myra starts looking her over, checking to make sure nothing is broken. Leah is just silent.

I'd rather have anything but her silence.

"Okay, sweetheart, one last question. Did he touch you some-where that made you uncomfortable?"

Leah's eyes widen. "Do you mean down there?" She looks toward her lap.

Myra nods.

She shakes her head. "He's never done anything like that. He just got mad and hit me."

I want to sink to the ground in relief.

"I'm going to take some blood, okay?" Myra looks at me for permission.

"Yes, of course." I walk over and hold Leah's hand as Myra takes her blood. She doesn't even flinch, and I'm sure this pain is nothing compared to the bruises on her face and stomach. I can tell some of the bruises are older than those inflicted tonight.

A few minutes later Myra is finished, and she leaves me and Leah alone. "Let me show you to your room. Tomorrow you and I will go shopping to get things for your room and whatever else you want."

She smiles. "Thank you, Gracie."

I laugh softly, loving seeing the real her. As I lead her upstairs, I pass Aiden, who is in the living room talking to Ryan. He's a member of the Devils Souls and Myra's husband.

I take Leah to the room beside Reid's, not the room where Aiden and I had sex earlier.

"Here you go." I push the door open and set her bag on the bed. I know one thing: she needs a whole new wardrobe; most of her clothes are very small on her. "Do you want to take a shower, while I fix you some food, before you take some meds for the pain?" I run my hand down her back. She looks a bit shell-shocked. "Towels are in the cabinets, soap and shampoo are too. Tomorrow we will get your own."

She nods and looks at the floor. I am sure she needs a few minutes alone so she can wrap her head around everything.

I don't like feeling powerless. I wish I could just take all of that away from her. "Just come downstairs whenever you're finished." I walk to the door.

"Thank you, Gracie, so much," she says and I turn around, smiling.

"You're more than welcome, sweetheart."

I gently shut the door behind me to give her privacy. One thing I loved when I had my new home was my privacy. I needed that so much. I needed that place where I felt safe, something to call my own.

Everyone has left and Aiden is locking up. He turns to look at me, and I'm suddenly so extremely exhausted.

"You okay, baby?" he asks, pulling me into his arms.

I nod and grip the back of his shirt, hugging him tightly. "I just want her to be happy. I'm so afraid that all of this is going to affect her life."

"No, baby. No. She is going to have you. We are going to make sure she is happy and thriving. She is going to have something that you didn't..."

I pull back and look at him, waiting for him to finish his sentence.

"She is going to have you."

"You're so damn sweet to me, Aiden." I kiss him softly before letting him hold me for a few minutes. I love feeling so safe in his arms; it's like everything outside of those arms just melts away.

"I need to fix her some food." I finally pull away and he follows me into the kitchen, where we make her a sandwich and a glass of milk.

"Her house didn't have anything but a box of crackers," he informs me.

"Luckily, the center fed her and sent food home." I am beyond thankful for that.

I hear the creak of the steps, and I anxiously wait for her to walk into the kitchen. She steps inside, her hair wet, in a pair of pajamas.

"Hi, honey. Do you want to eat in here or in the living room?" I ask her.

She thinks for a second. "Is the living room okay?"

"Of course!" I take the plate and her drink, and I follow her into the living room. I set the food on the coffee table.

Aiden comes out, a second later, with some pills. "Here's some Tylenol, honey." He sets it down for her.

We all sit down on the couch, and she is in the middle between me and Aiden. I can tell she is unsure.

"So do you want to watch *The Mummy*? It was my favorite show when I was your age."

"Really? I love that movie!"

I click on the TV.

She finishes all her food and settles in, her head lying against the back of the couch.

"Do you want a blanket?" Aiden asks her.

"Yes," she says timidly.

He takes the blanket off the back of the couch and lays it over her gently. She looks at him fully for the first time. I could tell that she was unsure of him.

Aiden does look a little scary with all of the tattoos and being a big guy, and it's natural for her to be wary of him after being beaten by her stepdad. But Aiden is just a big softy.

"Thank you," she says.

He smiles at her. "You're very welcome, sweetheart."

She returns his smile, and her little shoulders drop as some of her anxiety is lifted.

An hour into the movie, I notice her eyes closing every few seconds. She finally gives in and scoots over until she is lying against Aiden. I cover my mouth at the sight of his shocked face, and I try not to laugh. He pushes her hair out of her face.

"Do you want to carry her to her room?" I whisper softly so she doesn't wake up.

Aiden picks her up off the couch, and she clutches onto the

blanket and brings it up to her neck. Her eyes widen as she takes everything in. I make sure to reassure her of what is happening. "Aiden is carrying you to your room, honey. You fell asleep."

"Okay." She yawns, and I walk ahead of them to her bedroom and pull back the blankets.

Aiden gently lays her in her bed, covering her up. I love seeing how kind he is. He is a dad right down to his core and the very best kind.

She looks up at him and reaches out to take his hand. "Can you stay with me until I fall asleep?"

My heart warms. "I will go check on Reid."

Aiden

She wants me to stay with her, so I sit on the floor by her bed, still holding her hand. "You're scared?" I ask.

She nods. "I'm scared because this is different from everything I know."

"I bet it is, honey. Just know nothing will ever hurt you again. I will make sure of it."

She studies me for a minute. "I think I know that. I'm just sad because of my mommy. She left me."

My fucking heart breaks into a million pieces. I cannot fathom the thought of leaving Reid, and I can't stand the thought of leaving Leah.

I smooth her hair off her face. "I know she did, baby. I'm so sorry for that. I won't ever leave you, and Gracelyn won't either."

She nods and a tear falls down her face. I catch it and she smiles. She takes my hand and wraps both of hers around it. "I believe you. I think I'm going to be happy."

Fuck if I am not about to cry; this shit is so sad. "I will make sure of it, angel."

She closes her eyes, and her smile doesn't leave her face.

12

GRACE

WHEN I WAKE UP THE NEXT MORNING, AIDEN IS STILL ASLEEP. HE stayed with her for an hour last night, and I sat outside the door listening to them talk.

I love that she feels safe around him; I know the feeling all too well. Aiden just has a presence about him that makes you feel like everything is going to be okay.

I look at the clock on the wall—eight o'clock. I groan and rub my eyes, resting my face on Aiden's chest.

"What time is it?" he asks and I yawn.

"It's eight o'clock."

"Lane will be here in thirty minutes with all the paperwork."

Waiting for Lane is torture. I want to get all of this settled before someone comes along and tries to take Leah from me. I know that is not really possible though. If anyone in her family really cared about her well-being, they would have taken her in long before now. And she told me she has no family.

Lane knocks on the door before he steps inside the house. Reid has woken up already, and I'm cuddling him on the couch, feeding him a bottle.

Leah is still fast asleep. Before last night, I'm sure she hadn't slept well in a long time. If you're in a dangerous situation, you never fully rest. You're always alert and waiting.

Lane sets the papers on the coffee table, and he points to some lines. "Both of you sign here and sign here, and it will be final." I am beyond thankful for the MC connections at this moment. Aiden bends down and signs; then I shift Reid to my hip and sign too. Lane puts the papers in a folder, and he looks at both of us like he wants to say something.

"You're doing an amazing thing. It's going to take some adjusting. I remember the story of a woman Lane had dated hid Tiffany from him for years and years until she was finally discovered.

"We just want to make sure she has an amazing life. She deserves that," I say.

He looks upstairs. "She does...that shit should never happen. We are doing our best to make an impact when we can." I am proud of the way the MC tries to help those who need it. Lane shakes Aiden's hand and sees himself out.

"Have you guys ever thought of setting up an office of specialized people who can track, monitor, and then track down human trafficking operations?" I ask, shifting Reid to my other arm and patting his back. "I mean it would be fitting. They could reach further than just this town. Further than Texas."

Aiden looks at me for a few beats before grinning. "You know, that is an amazing idea." He takes out his phone and starts texting away.

Footsteps on the stairs bring me out of my thoughts, and I look up and see Leah.

"Good morning, honey, are you hungry?" I pat the couch next to me.

She sits down and stares at the coffee table in a complete daze. I rub her back gently. "Honey."

She finally looks at me. Her eyes are red and puffy; I can tell she has been crying for hours. I put Reid into his walker and pull her to my chest, and she latches onto me, crying.

Aiden comes back from the kitchen. He takes in the scene and slowly walks over and sits on Leah's other side. I want to cry right along with her; I hate this so much. I hate that she is still hurting. This is such a huge adjustment for her, and I'm sure she is so confused.

Aiden holds her hand and we sit in utter silence, aside from her crying and Reid smacking his hands on his toys.

Little by little, her crying slows, and she lifts her head off my chest. "Are you okay?" I help her dry her tears.

She nods, breathing deeply. "I'm sorry for crying like that." Her face reddens, and I can tell she is embarrassed.

Aiden touches her chin, getting her attention. "Never, ever be ashamed to show your emotions. There's nothing wrong with being sad, and there's nothing wrong with crying. Do what is needed for you and not others."

My poor heart can't handle any more of Aiden.

"I am not sad because I miss my own home. I'm happy because I thought, at first, that I dreamt that I got out of there. When I walked downstairs and saw Grace, it hit me that everything is better.

"Oh my sweetheart." I hug her and Aiden hugs me, resting his head on top of mine.

"How about we get dressed and all of us go out for breakfast before we go shopping?" I suggest and Leah's eyes light up.

"I would like that, Gracie." She runs upstairs and I lean back into the couch, relaxing for a moment.

"She is one tough little girl."

I nod. "It's time for her to be a little girl."

Leah

It feels like a dream; it's like I'm going to wake up any second and I'll be back at home. Last night, for the first time, I was not afraid. I used to be so scared to close my eyes, knowing he might barge into my room in a rage. He got mad at me over everything.

My mom was always passed out in the living room, from the drugs she had taken, and I would only come out of my room to go to school. I never even ate the food they had bought; I used the food I got from the center.

Now Grace said I am going shopping—I have never even been to the mall—and she mentioned getting breakfast. What would it be like to order any kind of food you want?

I am sitting on my new bed, in my own room with a lock and my own bathroom. I can shower without the fear of someone just walking in.

But, on the other hand, I am so scared. What if they get tired of me and just get rid of me?

That is my worst fear.

There's a knock on my door, and I walk over and open it. Grace and Aiden are standing there with some papers in their hands.

"Oh yeah, we forgot to tell you. We officially adopted you this morning."

"You mean?"

They nod and it hits me that they're not going to get rid of me. I am officially theirs, and there's no going back from it.

"I am going to get ready." I grin and shut the door, and I walk over to my bed, grab my pillow, and scream into it. I can't contain my excitement.

Grace

Leah's eyes are huge as she takes in everything at the mall. I can tell she is overwhelmed, but I love that she grabs Aiden's hand for comfort. It's the small things that really matter; she's letting me know that she trusts us.

After we told her that she was officially adopted, we could hear her squealing with excitement inside her room.

I am taking her into a kids' clothing store. Aiden is sitting outside the store on one of the dad couches.

Leah thumbs through every single one of the racks. She points to an outfit she likes, and we put it in the basket. Little by little, we have enough clothes for a brand-new wardrobe. We make sure to get accessories, undergarments, and toiletries for her.

I love the look on her face; it's like she is floating on air. She is staring at all her stuff in disbelief. I know how she is feeling. I remember when just getting a new outfit was a huge deal. All my clothes came from god knows where, and they were stained and full of holes. I am thankful for my grandparents, because I am able to live the life I live because of them.

I know that Aiden would happily pay for all of this but, after much arguing, he agreed to let me pay for the clothes. He insisted on handling everything else.

Next we will be getting things to decorate her room, a TV, and a cell phone—it's important for all the MC kids to have one in case of an emergency. Plus I know she secretly really wants to talk to Tiffany. She is excited about Tiffany coming over to practice softball.

"Tomorrow I have to go to the center. Do you still want to go?" I ask her, as we wait for everything to be rung up.

"I know that I don't have to be there anymore, but I still have friends that go there. I can help you help them." She is the absolute sweetest.

"Then it's settled." I press my palm to the top of her head, and she hugs me slightly.

The total comes up on the screen. "It's too much," Leah tells me and tries to put some of the stuff back.

"No, honey, this is just making up for all the things you never had," I tell her softly .

She agrees and I pay, and we walk out of the store with all our bags. Aiden is sitting on the couch looking beyond miserable. We were probably in there over two hours.

Reid is sitting in Aiden's lap, chewing on a teether. "How is my boy?" I ask and put my stuff down so I can pick him up and smother his face with kisses.

"Did you girls have fun?" Aiden asks Leah. He is such a trooper. Not many people would be completely fine sitting there for hours.

I put Reid back into his stroller. Aiden puts as many of the bags as he can in the compartment below the stroller, and he carries the rest.

See? This is why you bring guys along!

Leah is talking to Aiden every second about everything she got, including some biker boots.

"Biker boots, huh?" He winks at me, and she goes into detail explaining everything. "You want to be a biker one day?" he asks her, dead serious.

She rubs her arm with her thumb. I've noticed she does that when she is nervous. "I think so, but instead of carrying a gun I would like knives."

Aiden grins. "I think we can get you some knives so you can start practicing."

THE REST of the day was a complete blur. We spent the whole day together, leaving our phones in the vehicle to avoid interruptions.

Now Leah is in bed, Reid is asleep, and Aiden and I are lying together, watching TV. I'm exhausted.

"Tomorrow I am going after your uncle." Aiden is trailing his finger up and down my arm.

I stare at the wall and ask myself *why am I okay with this?* But I know that everything happens for a reason, and I am the way I am because it's meant to be that way.

"Okay," I say simply.

I hold no real feelings toward these people but complete and utter hatred. I am not someone who generally hates people, but I hate them.

Just the thought of my father makes me so sick to my stomach. When I was younger and still lived outside the city, I would pass him on the highway. I wanted so badly to push him off the road. I thought of many different ways to kill him.

"You're okay with this?" Aiden rolls me over onto my back so he is looking down at me.

I bite my bottom lip for a second. "I'm fine with it." I drag my hand from his shoulder to his forearm. "I have wanted both of them to suffer for a long time."

Over the years I barely remembered the details—until I got older and then, little by little, it started to come to me. When I was twenty-one I got to the point I was depressed and anxious all the time. I went to a therapist and that changed my life. I told them every single detail, and it was the most freeing experience of my life. But I still had issues with being touched until I met Aiden.

He just had ways of making me feel so safe—all those walls just drifted down. "My uncle touched my cousins too but, as far as I know, I was the only kid my father did all of that to."

He closes his eyes, his jaw tight. I haven't really given him that much detail because, honestly, it makes me feel embarrassed. I shouldn't feel that way, but the instinct to feel shame is real. But now I need to let everything out. If Aiden is going to make them suffer, he needs to know all the details.

I go into more depth about everything that happened to me sexually, verbally, and physically. Carrying all of this inside has been hard. Talking to therapists helped me a ton, but speaking to someone I love is different; it's so much more personal.

My fear that no one could love me ran deep. I knew Aiden wouldn't leave me but, nonetheless, the fear is still there.

He listens while I tell him all my fears and insecurities and, in the end, he just holds me and tells me I'm absolutely beautiful, strong, and amazing.

Aiden
The next day

I am standing outside her uncle's place, and the guys are surrounding the house. There is no escaping, especially since I found out that Grace was not the only girl he abused.

We allowed him to grieve for a day or two after his wife's funeral. Not that this was necessary. He has no soul. He is probably the one who put her in the hospital. Her medical records state the cause of death was blunt force trauma to her head.

It hurts Grace that the only person in that family who cared for her died this way. She wanted Mary to get out of that family.

"Come out, come out, wherever you are!" I taunt, waiting for him to come outside. One big mistake he made was living right in the middle of nowhere. This makes our job so much easier.

A minute passes and the door opens, little by little, until I can see him standing in the doorframe. "You know why I'm here," I tell him.

He pales and raises his hands. "Why don't you just leave me alone? My wife just died."

I roll my eyes. Does he think using her is really going to work? "We let you have a few days to grieve, and we both know how she really died, don't we?"

He drops his sad expression, knowing he's been caught red-handed, and he steps further out onto the porch. My hands are itching to be wrapped around his neck. I want to choke the fucking life out of him, and I would enjoy every second of it.

"Is the bitch really worth it?" he asks.

I see red and, beside me, Wilder laughs. "Do you *want* to fucking die?" he says. He is surely asking for it.

"Get your ass down, you have two options."

He walks down the stairs, like he isn't seconds away from having his life taken from him. He stands in front of me cockily. I hate him so fucking much.

"First I want you to call your brother. I want you to tell him that I'm coming for him." He starts to argue, and I smash my fist into his mouth. "Do as I fucking ask!" I yell in his face.

He slowly takes out his phone and dials the number. His eyes connect with mine, and I know his brother answered. "I have a message for you," he starts and I nod, telling him to go on. "Aiden wants you to know that he is coming for you." He hangs up, and I take the phone and throw it to the ground.

"You have two options, you can die or I take your hands." I'm not fucking sugarcoating anything.

His eyes widen as it sinks in that I mean fucking business, and he looks around like he is trying to figure out a way to get out of it. He swallows hard, sweat pouring off his face, because he realizes he is stuck.

"It sucks being trapped and scared, doesn't it?" I am loving seeing him ready to piss his pants.

"Look man, I was young and dumb."

I shake my head. "I heard that you did things to other girls too, it wasn't just my woman. You knew what you were doing, and it's time to face your sins."

I grip his face. "Now, hands or die." I let his face go, causing his head to snap back.

He swallows hard. "Hands."

We brought a doctor with us. He will make sure Grace's uncle doesn't die from his wounds, and one of the prospects will drop him off at the hospital. He will never touch anyone else. Her father will not get an option. He is going straight to fucking hell.

One of the prospects drags out a table, and Grace's uncle starts to shake.

"I want you to remember, she was scared and she was stuck. The other girls were scared, and everything was out of their control. You are hopeless, you're trapped. You will never fucking feel fear and helplessness to the extent they did, but you will suffer. You hurt your wife, you killed her. You deserve fucking more, but I take great pleasure in knowing that you will suffer for the rest of your life."

I kick his legs out from under him, and he lands on his knees. Logan grabs his arm and stretches it out across the table. I am handed an axe and Logan nods at me, trusting that I won't hit him. Grace's uncle starts to scream, hiding his face.

Logan holds the uncle's hand, and I lift the axe and slam it down as hard as I can. Logan falls back as the hand detaches from the arm. Travis catches him, and I sever the other hand. The doctor steps in and does whatever is needed before the prospect takes him to the emergency room.

I throw the axe to the ground by his face. Logan sets one of his hands on his porch like it's a fucking decoration.

I do not feel regret; sick fucks like this deserve it.

A vehicle pulls in, and I smile as I realize it's her father. I wiggle my finger, grinning. He is next, but it's not going to happen just yet. I want him to be terrified, waiting for me to pop up. When he least expects it, it'll happen.

Let the games begin.

13

GRACE

A month later

"LET'S GO, GIRLS!" I SCREAM AS THEY RUN AROUND THE BASES. WE
are about to secure the state championship, and if we win we will
be hitting the nationals.

One of the girls dives for the ball, and Leah jumps over her
and slides into home.

We won!

I throw my clipboard and run onto the field to my girls. We
have worked and trained so hard. Leah and Tiffany have trained
every single day, at each other's houses, in addition to team practice. They are determined to be the best in the world.

And it paid off—we won with flying colors. They all fall onto
each other and I laugh; they're so excited. Aiden laughs as Leah
jumps up and down. The grin on her face is one of pure
happiness.

This past month I have seen such an amazing change in her.
She has settled into her new life, and she becomes happier
every day.

Therapy has been a huge help to her. Braelyn, her therapist, works with the Devils Souls MC often. She is a sweetheart and Leah loves her. Aiden and Ethan, who is Braelyn's husband, have become good friends on top of that. Ethan is a police officer, but he is cool with the MC because they helped rescue his sister a couple of years ago.

Tiffany and Leah are doing a handshake they made up. I love the fact that they're such close friends.

"This is utter bullshit!!" someone yells, and one of the parents throws a water bottle at the girls.

What the...? I look at Aiden in disbelief. *I understand you're upset your child has lost, but that doesn't mean you should act like an ass.*

I walk over to the fence. "Ma'am, can you please not throw things?" I don't want trouble, but that is uncalled for.

She looks at me, and I can tell that I made a mistake in approaching her. But I'd rather her attention be on me than on the girls.

The guy sitting next her gets up, and all I can think is *uh oh.* "You have a problem, bitch?" He charges down the metal bleachers.

"You better not be talking to my woman." Aiden has handed Reid off to Leah, who is staring at me. I smile at her reassuringly.

"Look, there are kids around." My trying to defuse the situation just makes the guy madder. He walks around the fence until he is face to face with me, and the woman who started it all charges right behind him.

Oh joy.

Aiden is at my side in a split second. He gently pushes me back and moves in front of me. "Look fucker, you need to turn around and get behind that fence before I beat the shit out of you," Aiden says in a hushed tone. "It's a game. Kids are around, and I am sure you're embarrassing your daughter."

The guy wouldn't stand a chance against Aiden, who is at

least twice his size. He looks at both of us before backing away and practically dragging the woman from the dugout.

Aiden shakes his head. "People are literally dumb."

I have to agree. I have seen upset parents many times, but I have never been threatened before—that's a new one.

Leah runs over.

"You did so amazing today, sweetheart!" I hug her and she hugs me back, jumping in my arms with excitement.

"I can't believe we are going to the nationals!" she screams. She hugs Aiden and we both laugh.

She has brightened up our lives so much; she is an angel. Always laughing and happy-go-lucky. She is so resilient.

Amelia and Lane walk over to us. "Want to take all the girls out to pizza before we drive back home?"

"I love that idea. Tell the girls, sweetheart?" I ask her and she runs over to them.

"What happened with the parents?" Lane asks. They're standing at the opposite end of the field, glaring at both of us.

"They didn't like losing." I try to ignore their stares. All the kids pile into the bus. Aiden is driving behind us, because the bus isn't exactly car seat approved, and Lane is riding with Aiden. Amelia sits down beside me, and we start singing a song with the girls. It makes me so happy to see the excitement on their faces. Most of these kids don't have much enjoyment in their lives. I even see a huge difference in Tiffany since she and Leah have gotten so close.

Someone blows their horn loudly and swerves toward us before speeding away. My heart is in my chest. I look behind us at the girls; their faces are glued to the windows.

"It's okay, girls, return to your seats."

They all sit down, and the crazy driver is instantly forgotten.

～

WE JUST FINISHED OUR FOOD, and I am holding the door open for the girls. Lane is standing at the bus, and Aiden is inside paying for it all. Amelia helps the girls get seated.

We are an hour from our town. When we arrive, the girls will be dropped off at school, where someone will pick them up.

"Well, if it isn't the bitch of a coach?" someone says. It's woman from earlier who was mad they lost.

Are you kidding me?

"There is a bunch of kids around, can you please not do this?" I ask her and let the door shut.

She laughs. "Of course I am going to do this. You have a smart mouth." She moves closer, until I can smell her and feel her breath on my face. It's rancid, that's for sure. I pinch my lips together so I don't vomit right in her face. I think it's been a long time since she bathed, and half her teeth are missing or cracked in half. I have a huge inkling that she is on something, and that's what's causing her to act so rashly, but what do I know? It could just be her beautiful personality.

What do I do? I don't want to get into a fight with this woman, because the kids are nearby, on the bus. "Please, what would this settle?" I ask her, and she bursts out laughing, causing spit to fly everywhere. Luckily, I dodge it.

She grins—*I wouldn't do that if I were you.* "How about I go tell all the kids what kind of bitch you are." She takes out a knife.

Oh, hell no. I see red. She starts to run across the parking lot, and I catch up to her easily. She's not even running. It's just a bit faster than her sluggish walk.

I grab her by the hair, making her head snap back and causing her to fall on her ass. "Look, you can do whatever the fuck you want to me, but don't ever threaten these kids."

Lane runs over. "What the fuck is going on?" he asks, and I explain what she is trying to do.

"Bitch, you better get your ass out of here before my wife finds out what you're doing," Lane growls at her, his fists clenched.

I would do whatever it takes to protect those I care about but, honestly, I am not a fighter unless I have to be. This woman just needs to get the fuck out of here before I lose my temper and make her eat concrete.

"What the fuck?" Aiden asks, still holding Reid. I take the baby from Aiden so he can deal with this woman.

"Grace, what is happening?" Leah asks from the steps of the bus.

I smile at her reassuringly. "Nothing is wrong, sweetheart. Why don't you and Tiffany watch a movie on the iPad?"

She slowly takes in the scene before she disappears into the bus.

The woman is still lying on the ground like I just beat the shit out of her or something. She looks up at us, her eyes wide, before she starts screaming at the top of her lungs and rolls, on the ground, toward Amelia. Lane snatches her up off the ground, and she starts to scratch her skin.

"What is going on?" I ask Aiden.

"Let me call an ambulance." Lane takes out his phone, and I watch in horror as the woman takes off at a dead run across the parking lot.

"She is going to hurt herself." She is already too close to traffic. I start to go after her.

She stops suddenly and turns around; then she grins and takes out the knife. She raises it maniacally, reminding me of Chucky, and runs toward us, screaming at the top of her lungs.

Aiden lifts me inside the bus, and Lane does the same with Amelia.

The lady tries to run into the bus. The girls start screaming, and I slam the doors closed as Lane pulls her back by her hair. She hits the ground with a smack. Her arm is lying at funny angle, but she gets right up and runs face-first into the door.

Is this the zombie apocalypse or something?

"Gracie!" Leah calls and I open my arms for her. She buries

her face into my chest as I hug her tightly. Tiffany is doing the same with Amelia.

The woman jabs the knife toward the bus windows. "Close the windows!" I tell the girls, and they hurry to do as I ask. Luckily, the windows are too high for her to reach, but I don't want to take the chance of her throwing something inside.

Aiden and Lane hold her down until the ambulance comes; it's the longest five minutes of my life.

Amelia looks at me, pale. "A new drug is on the street," she whispers. Clearly, it's dangerous, and someone needs to put a stop to it.

~

Grace
The next day

WE HAVE DECIDED to stay inside the house today and relax after such an exhausting night. Leah is lying in the floor with Reid, playing with some of his toys.

That lady was in horrible shape last night. I stood next to Aiden as the paramedic told him this was the fifth call that night to people in this condition. It's scary to think that a drug can make someone completely lose their mind. I mean she didn't even blink—it was that bad. And she laughed and rolled around on the ground like she was possessed.

There's a beep at the gate. "I think it's the grocery man." We just ordered some ingredients for lasagna, which I have been majorly craving all day. I yell for Aiden, and I look at the security screen on the wall. I push a button to let the delivery man through the gate, and he does an absolutely weird thing. He stops just inside the gate, gets out of his car, and walks toward our house.

Aiden walks into the living room with cash for a tip. He looks at the camera and his brow furrows. "Why is he walking?" He is shuffling along with his head hanging down, and his cap is pushed down close to his eyes.

Okay, this is very sketchy.

Aiden opens the door and steps out onto the front porch. I stand at the entrance waiting on him. The man walks up our drive and I wave at Logan, who is sitting on his porch with a beer. He waves back. Note to self: invite him over for dinner.

The delivery guy sets the groceries on the porch, and I bend down to pick them up just as I hear a snap.

Aiden

Something is not right about this—the hair on the back of my neck is standing up. Something is up with the delivery guy.

He sets the groceries down on the porch. He doesn't say a word but continues to look down.

What the fuck?

Gracie bends over and tries to pick up one of the bags. That's when his head shoots up, and I see his grin and the fork in his hand. He raises his hand to stab Gracelyn. I grip his hand and twist it, breaking it instantly.

Gracelyn backs away and looks at him in horror. The stupid fucker tried to stab her in the head.

I grip him by the throat and drag him off the porch. I put my foot on his throat, and he goes batshit crazy like the woman last night. Logan runs over to me and, one by one, all the guys who live in the area follow.

Gracelyn is sitting on the stairs, her eyes filled with fear because she could have died.

I am pissed right the fuck off. This drug issue is going to cause a lot of problems unless we stop it.

Lane rolls up on his bike as Logan is tying up the delivery guy. "We have a big problem," I tell Lane and the others. "We need a fucking meeting. I just got a call from the chief because this is too much for them to handle. A police officer is on his way to get this guy, and then we head to the club."

The fucker is rolling around on the ground laughing, his arms tied behind him. He kicks his legs up in the air, and it makes me fucking sick.

"Come here, honey." I motion to Gracelyn, and she runs over and buries her face in my chest. It fucking kills me that she was scared, that the fucker came right up to my front door and tried this.

The police come and take him away, kicking and screaming.

"All the women, go inside the house and hit the code red button. It will completely lock down the houses. We have prospects at the gate, and we will electrify it. No one is getting on that fucker unless they want to be fried."

I help Gracelyn into the house. "I will be home later, baby. You know how to alert the system, correct?"

She nods but I can tell she is worried.

I push her hair out of her face, cupping her jaw. "I will put a stop to it, honey. Relax and spend time with the kids. Nothing is getting in." I kiss her forehead.

She lets out a deep breath. "Be safe, okay?"

"Always." I kiss her on the lips.

I walk over to my kids. I kiss Leah on the top of her head and then Reid. "I will be home in a couple of hours." Leah nods, going back to texting Tiffany.

I walk to the door, kissing Grace one more time before I step outside, where Logan is waiting on me. I hear the groans as the steel windows and doors snap into place. No one can get into the house unless they're let in. Our tech guy will be monitoring the whole property and alarming it.

Nothing is going to hurt them. Usually if it's something extra dangerous we go to the clubhouse and go on lockdown.

We are going to drive our trucks because it's safer; we don't want to get shot on the way to the clubhouse by all the crazies.

It's BAD. We watch the video: people are running all over town blown out of their minds. When the drugs wear off, they go back to normal, but while they're high, they're unpredictable.

"Apparently this drug is the cheapest on the market outside of weed, but it's the most dangerous," Lane explains. We watch as a woman leaving a grocery store is charged by one of the workers. She manages to get in her vehicle before she is hit with a watermelon.

"What are we going to do?" I ask Lane, not taking my eyes off the commotion happening all over the city.

"I am in the process of tracking down the source, and once that happens we will destroy the operation."

Smiley slams his hand on the table. "Did it hit Raleigh?" His daughter and son-in-law live there, along with Smiley's step-daughter, Alisha. Lane looks at his phone and nods.

"I just got a text from Kyle. He was telling me that he just got a call about a crazy running around downtown naked," Lane says.

I lean back in my chair, my hands behind my head. "Jeez." What the fuck is this shit, and how did it spread so quickly?

"All I can tell you is to go home. I am waiting for a phone call about the location, and Randy is checking all the cameras in town, trying to pinpoint where it's flowing from." Lane sits down, and none of us moves as a woman runs through town, wearing only a pair of underwear on her head, laughing.

"Everyone in the gated community tonight, phones ready. I

should get the call tonight or in the morning. Prospects will be lined up all across the property for extra safety."

We all file out of the clubhouse, going to our vehicles. There is no one on the streets but a few people who are on the new drug. They run right in front of our vehicles, throw rocks at us, and try to head butt our windows whenever we stop.

Logan voices what I'm thinking. "Fuck man, this shit is bad."

Up ahead I see a woman trying to break into a car and hear a scream come from within the vehicle. I screech to a stop, and Logan hops out and tears the woman away from the car. I hold her down on the ground, not wanting to hurt her. Logan opens the car door, and the woman inside has blood pouring down her face. "Come with me," he says. "I can patch you up. It's not safe." He hovers over her as he puts her in his vehicle. I let the woman on the ground go and hurry back to my truck.

Logan has already dug out gauze from the first aid kit that I keep in the truck. "Did she hit you in the head?" He tilts her head side to side, and I have to hide my grin.

Logan fusses over her the whole way home, and she is smiling the whole time. She's completely smitten with him if I have any say in it.

She is the polar opposite of him. She is tiny with long blond hair, blue eyes, and a pale complexion. Logan has dark hair and dark brown eyes and is really tan.

I drop them off at his house, and he practically carries her inside, as if her legs were damaged rather than her head.

I laugh and call Grace. "Let me in, angel."

She raises the metal door, and I walk inside to find them all cuddled up on the couch. I was gone longer than I thought, and now it's almost time for them to go to bed.

Gracelyn scoots over and makes room for me on the arm of the chair. Leah is leaning against her side, and Reid is sitting in her lap, content with playing with his toys.

"I missed my babies." I touch Reid's and Leah's heads, and

Leah looks up at me, flashing that beautiful smile of hers. We have gotten close. It took a couple of days for her to warm up to me, because she has never had a strong male figure in her life. If we're really being honest, she never had a mother figure either. She told me that her mom was high every single day. She would sober up for like a week, but then she turned back to drugs and needed boyfriends to help her get by. Leah and her mother were often homeless. They spent nights under bridges. Her mother would shoot up or smoke as she slept.

We put Leah in intensive therapy, and it's helped her tremendously. Leah is a strong little girl, and I am so proud of the progress she has made.

My mother is dating Walker, and I am fucking thrilled. Yeah, right, it's strange seeing my mother dating, because I can't honestly remember her doing that until now.

I sit on the couch, safe in our house, while the outside world has completely gone to shit. I have a huge feeling this is going to get worse before it gets better. It's spreading from one town to the next.

Grace
A couple of days later

I am in the pick-up line with Aiden, waiting for Leah to get out of school. I know one thing: I was incredibly nervous about letting her go.

The drug epidemic has gotten worse. The downtown area is practically a ghost town, because that's where it runs rampant. The police department has done a lot to keep it isolated, but when they close one dealer down, three more pop up.

I am scared.

I've seen people rolling around on the side of the road. Our gated community is safe, and Lane has left the prospects at the women's disposal so we can have protection if we have to go out and our men are busy. But I worry for others who don't have that much security.

We have practice after school, and we are picking up Tiffany while we're at it because Lane is so busy with the drug problem.

Raleigh, Texas, the Devils Souls town, has been hit just as hard, and the surrounding towns are slowly getting hit. I feel like all of Texas is going to be covered in this before the end.

Leah and Tiffany walk out of school together. I hop out of the car and hold the back door open for them as Aiden keeps watch.

The MC hired security for the school, but I didn't feel that Leah was safe there. So we've had it locked down, with guards at every entrance.

I get back in my seat. We have to drive a mile down the road to the softball field. I hand the girls their snacks. "Here girls."

I love this. I've always wanted to be a mom and take care of others the way I should have been take care of. I love Reid; it feels like he is my son. Leah is my daughter. Before my eyes my life has changed so much, but for the better. I see so much of myself in Leah; she truly is my daughter. She smiles a little more every day, and laughs a little more, and that just makes everything in life so worth it.

Aiden kisses the back of my hand. "You're beautiful. Have I told you that today?"

I smile. He is so incredibly cheesy sometimes, but I love that about him. I love every part of him, if I'm being honest. It feels like a dream, but it's one I never want to wake up from.

I was healed in so many ways before I met Aiden, but he healed the rest of me and I am happy. It's a deep-in-my-soul kind of happy that I'd only dreamed of having.

But I'm living it.

Aiden parks at the softball field. I climb out, and Leah hands me Reid from his car seat. "Your bags are in the back," Aiden tells them as he pulls out the stroller for Reid to relax in.

Leah and Tiffany get straight to work setting up for practice today. We'll be practicing our batting and offense. We have another game later this week, so the best thing for them is to play against each other. It'll be a tough game because they're all good. I split Tiffany and Leah up because—let's be honest—they are, hands down, the top two on the team.

I snuggle Reid against my chest. He is sucking on his hand, sleepy. It's kind of chilly today—in the sixties—and it will get colder as the sun goes down.

When the bus shows up with the rest of the girls, I take a blanket out of Reid's diaper bag and bundle him up like a little burrito. Aiden chuckles and rubs Reid's chubby cheek. "He likes to snuggle." The stroller will be relatively useless—I want to hold him all the time because I know there will come a day when he won't want me to.

Aiden kisses the side of my head. "I love you," I tell him and he smiles so beautifully.

"I love you, sweet girl." He looks around before he smacks me on the ass.

I laugh and walk closer to the field. "Okay girls, two teams. Tiffany has first choice, and then Leah chooses."

I move away and let them make the decisions. We have practiced so much they practically handle it all themselves.

I hope we win the nationals. They have worked so hard, and they want it so badly. I have seen them with broken fingers, and they come back the next day, slip off the splint, and have at it. Tiffany and Leah shake hands before running off, grinning.

"Those girls are trouble." Aiden chuckles. I have to agree, but the competition is totally healthy.

For the next hour we practice, and since it's getting really cold I allow them to go home early. Reid is asleep on my shoulder; he was out minutes after the girls started practicing. From the corner of my eye, I notice someone walking through the parking lot as the girls file onto the bus.

Tiffany is picking up the balls and storing them in the dugout while Leah puts away the bats. One second Leah is laughing with Tiffany—the next she is screaming. Her stepfather is flat-out sprinting toward her.

I cover my mouth so I don't scream. Aiden is next to her in a split second, catching her stepfather before he can reach her.

"Come here," I tell the girls, and Leah wraps her arms around my waist. "It's okay, sweetheart," I tell her soothingly. I can feel her shaking hard.

I want to fucking hurt him. How dare he do this to her?

He starts to scream and roll around on the ground. Fuck, he is on the drugs that are turning everyone insane, and he was already crazy.

"Let's get inside the truck." I take Leah's hand and lead her past Aiden, who is holding her stepfather down on the ground. He claws the ground as if he wants to get closer to us. "Leah!!" he screams in a weird high-pitched voice. It's like he is possessed.

Leah gets inside the truck, and she takes Reid from me and sets him in his seat. I look at her, concerned. Her hands are shaking, and her eyes are filled with tears as she stares at the back of the seat.

"Baby, he is nothing to you. He is not going to hurt you, and he is not going to take you away from me," I tell her softly, rubbing her back.

Tiffany takes her hand and holds it. "That's right, Leah. You're my sister and nobody hurts my sister."

How fucking amazing was that? I mouth "thank you" to Tiffany.

Leah sniffs and rubs her eyes, ridding herself of her tears. "It just scared me because he came out of nowhere."

"I know, honey. It's a scary thing."

I hear a very loud scream, and I turn around to see another crazy person running down the road toward us. I look at Aiden, who is tying Leah's stepdad up, and I slam the door shut and run over to him. I click the clicker to make sure nobody gets inside the vehicle. "Aiden, there's another one!"

It's another guy and he looks rough, like he has been running for days and days. He is emaciated, and I don't think he is going to make it long.

Aiden jumps up, takes my hand, and leads me back toward the truck. The guy is still a softball field away from us, but I want to be miles away. Aiden opens his door, and I climb over to the passenger seat, hitting the lock button on my door. I lean over the seat and buckle Reid in. Aiden shuts his door just as the crazy runs headfirst into our window. Blood splatters across the window as he does it over and over again. He grins, and his teeth are completely bloody.

"Aiden, something is not right," I whisper.

He puts the vehicle in reverse, and it bumps as we run over the crazy's foot. Aiden speeds back toward the main highway, and I look back to see the crazy trying his best to run after us.

We sit in silence as we try to wrap our heads around what happened. I look at Aiden. He is beyond pissed off. His hands are gripping the steering wheel so hard I can hear it cracking.

"Gracelyn, I'm not sure what just happened," Leah says from the back seat.

I'm not sure what to say because I'm clueless myself. This drug epidemic is getting out of hand, and I'm just confused as to how it got to this point.

Aiden takes out his phone and talks to Lane, explaining everything that happened. Tiffany is silent in the back seat.

I just don't know what to think.

From outside the car, so many people are going about their normal lives, but then we see someone who is blown out of their mind. People are going to get hurt—people are going to die—if something is not done about all of this.

But how do we do it? I know the MC is investigating it, but it's weird how it just came from absolutely nowhere.

Aiden pulls to a stop outside the gate, puts the code in, and drives in, the gates slamming shut behind us. Lane is sitting in our driveway with Amelia.

Lane opens the door and pulls his daughter out, hugging her. Tiffany closes her eyes, and I know she has been wanting her family. I want to take Leah inside, hold her, and make sure she is okay. I worry that this is going to be a setback for her. She doesn't need any of that.

I open her door, and she already has Reid out of his seat. I take him and help her out. Aiden is explaining what happened to Lane and Amelia. I take her inside the house and set Reid in his playpen.

Leah runs upstairs and into the shower. What do I do? I sit on the couch and cover my face, as the stress is overwhelming. It's really fucking scary out there right now, and I'm not sure when it's going to get better.

A few minutes later Aiden walks into the house and sits down next to me. I curl into his side, immediately feeling safe.

"How is she?" he asks, rubbing my arm.

"I think it really shook her up to see him acting like a complete savage. It's like her nightmare came true," I whisper.

Aiden tightens his grip on me. "I should have killed him before, and none of this would have happened."

I sit up and look at him. "Do not blame yourself! It's all his fault." How dare he blame himself for something like that. Leah's stepfather did this to himself. No one forced them to take the drug, and no one forced him to be abusive.

An hour later Aiden's phone rings, and as he listens to the person on the other end, he grins.

"We have them," he tells me and runs out of the house. I go to key pad on the wall and lock down the house.

Aiden

We sit outside a huge warehouse thirty minutes outside of town. Lane found out that a cartel wants to use our town as their prime base. There are vehicles outside, and I can see people standing in front of the windows cooking the shit.

Logan and Wilder are at the back to make sure no one escapes.

We walk down to the fucking warehouse like we own it. I open the door, and we run inside with our guns raised.

"I want every one of you fuckers outside in ten seconds, or I will blow your fucking faces off," Lane roars and everyone takes off running.

The smell inside is one that I can't describe. It's like they're taking every single drug known to man and combining them.

The back door opens, and Logan comes in and sets down the bomb. We are about to fucking blow this place to bits.

We all walk outside to our vehicles, which are far enough away that we won't be affected by the blast. The workers from inside are running down the dirt road, trying to get away, and I hope that they tell their boss. I want them to know we're coming for them and we will find them.

Logan runs up the hill and hands Lane the remote. He clicks the button and the warehouse explodes. I can feel the heat across my skin as the flames reach far into the sky. We all watch in silence as this one is taken down. It was filled with drugs.

This will cripple them.

We will find the next and the next until we find the person who caused this. Then they will have a bullet in their head.

14

GRACE

A few weeks later

I SIT ON THE EDGE OF THE TUB, STARING AT THE SMALL STICK IN MY hand that's going to change my life. I've been feeling really bad in the mornings, and the food cravings have been wild.

For the heck of it I decided to take a pregnancy test, but not for one second did I think it would be positive.

But here I am staring at the word *pregnant* on the digital screen. Aiden is in our bedroom because its eight o'clock in the morning and the kids will be up any minute. I set the test on the tub and splash cold water on my face, trying to focus my mind.

Will Aiden be upset? Will he think it's too much? Reid is still a baby, and we have Leah.

"Are you okay in there?" he calls through the door, and I dry my face, trying to think of what to say. I open the door and he looks at me. "Are you okay?" he asks again.

I smile reassuringly. "Yeah, I'm fine."

He gives me a look that lets me know he doesn't believe me, and he walks into the bathroom. As he turns on the shower he pauses, looking at the bathtub. I forgot the pregnancy test was sitting on the edge of the tub. He picks it up for a closer look.

My heart is in my throat. I should have had some cute way to tell him or something.

Not like this.

I lick my lips, twisting my hands together nervously, just waiting for him to say something.

He finally turns around after what seems like hours. "You're...?" he starts and then stops. Tears stream down my face; he is smiling so beautifully. "You're pregnant." He picks me up and sets me on the edge of the sink, hugging me. "I am so fucking happy, baby," he says softly, resting his face on my shoulder.

"I need to make sure. We need to go to the doctor." I run my fingers down his face.

He pulls back smiling and kisses my forehead. "Okay, I will call a doctor right now."

I smile and we cuddle for a few more moments. I feel dumb for worrying for even a split second. I can't wait to tell Leah. She absolutely loves Reid, and she is always ready to hold him.

"YOU'RE pregnant with one hundred percent certainty," the doctor says as we all look at the small bean on the screen. The sound of the heartbeat fills me with relief and happiness beyond imagining.

Aiden is holding my hand, stroking my fingers. He hasn't stopped smiling since he found out, and neither have I.

"The babies look fine."

Wait, did she just say...? I look at Aiden, wide eyed. "Did you just say?" I ask her and she laughs.

"Yes, I said babies. You have two." She points to the screen, and that's when I see the other little bean.

I have been so blessed, with not just one baby but two.

Aiden kisses my forehead before resting his head against mine. Together, in this moment, we let it sink in that we are going to be parents to two kids.

"Four," I whisper, my stomach filled with butterflies.

He laughs. "Four," he repeats. "Damn, I have got some super swimmers," he jokes and I gently smack his chest. That is such a guy thing to say.

The doctor laughs and hands me some papers along with a prescription for prenatal vitamins. Aiden holds the door open for me, and we walk out into the parking lot.

Everything has completely died down with the drugs. Whatever Aiden and the guys did, it put a stop to it. There have been a few more incidents, but not like it was a couple of weeks ago.

"I could really go for a juicy burger right now and some fries." My mouth is watering at the thought of the burger.

Aiden laughs. "Why do I have a feeling that I will be making a lot of late-night snack runs?"

Before I can answer, I see my father standing outside a store staring at us. My hands are shaking as I grip Aiden's hand. I look up to tell him, but he is already eyeing my father. Why is he here? It can't be a coincidence that he's outside the place we just left.

Aiden opens the door and helps me inside the vehicle, slamming the door shut, and he charges across the parking lot. My father runs away from Aiden, who stops and watches him leave. My heart is racing, and vomit is ready to crawl up my throat.

I am not going to let him ruin my high; that's for sure. I am pregnant with twins. I touch my belly. It's hard to imagine that they're growing inside me.

Aiden gets inside the truck, and he is pissed. His jaw is clenched, his eyes darkened. "Fucking pussy," he growls.

"I'm just confused as to why he was there."

Aiden relaxes his hand and intertwines our fingers. "I don't know, baby, but it won't matter much longer."

I know what that means. I know that he has something

planned for my father. I don't want to know the details, but I will rest easy knowing that he is out of my life. For so many years I was so afraid he would show up and do god knows what. He is literally psycho. He used to kill my animals so I wouldn't say anything; then it just got to the point that he was killing for the heck of it. That's when I did what I had to do to get out.

He always tried to have the upper hand with me. He would randomly show up at my softball games, and I would run for the bus. He would watch, smiling, as it drove away.

After those moments, I had so much fear in my heart that I just went through the motions of day-to-day life in a daze.

For years I was numb, trying to forget.

Then I turned twenty-one and everything changed. It all started hitting me at once, and the fear and depression affected my everyday life.

I wasn't going to let him win by continuing to have power over me. I took my fate in my own hands and went into intense therapy. It was not easy—none of it was easy—but it was worth it.

I look over at Aiden. He is a sign that I'm moving on and living my life. I was scared to be with him—no, I was terrified. I was terrified of being alone but, at the same time, I was scared to be in a close relationship. But then I pushed through that and threw caution to the wind. It was the best decision I have ever made.

I am so happy. I am right-down-to-my-very-core happy. I go to sleep happy, and I wake up even happier because I am surrounded by those I love.

We return to his house—I should probably say it's mine too. I am not sure what to do with my house. I haven't really been there since I met Aiden.

Laurie is waiting for us at the door, and right behind her is Walker. Aiden growls under his breath at the sight of him. I try not to laugh, because it's been weeks now and it hasn't gotten any easier for him. Walker is absolutely head over heels for Laurie.

"Well, are you?" She is practically bouncing with excitement.

Aiden grins widely. I know he beyond proud that we're having twins. It must be a man thing.

"Yes, with two." He gloats and I laugh at Laurie's expression. She looks down at my stomach and then at my face. "Two," she whispers.

"Yes."

She throws her arms up and starts screaming, and she runs over and hugs me, crying. "I will have four grand-babies," she says between her sobs.

I try not to cry, but this is an amazing moment. Leah steps out onto the porch, smiling. Laurie holds up two fingers. I nod and Leah runs over to Aiden and hugs him. He picks her up like she's a small child and hugs her tightly.

I love the relationship they have. She is always attached to his hip from the moment he gets home. They go fishing, and he teaches her how to change a tire and shoot a gun.

"I think they'll be boys," Leah says, grinning and still hugging Aiden, who is eating it up.

I touch my stomach. "I'm fine with whatever God gives me."

Laurie hugs me again before Walker pulls her away into his arms. She rolls her eyes. "I was hugging her."

He shrugs. "Those are my hugs. I share you for a bit, and then it's time for you to get back where you belong." He kisses the top of her head, smirking. Laurie just grins and I know she loves it.

Aiden, on the other hand, is glaring at both of them. "Can you guys chill the fuck out in front of me?"

Walker grins, turns her around, and kisses her passionately. I have to look away and Leah hides her eyes.

"I'm going to kill him," Aiden growls and sets Leah down.

"Aiden." Laurie gives him the mom look, and he walks into the house, pissed off. Not able to hold it in anymore, I burst out laughing. She joins in, and together we walk arm in arm into the house.

Walker is leaning against the wall, grinning, his arms crossed. He is totally trying to get on Aiden's nerves for the hell of it.

Laurie smacks him gently on the chest. "Behave, Walker."

He pulls her to his chest. "That's not what you said last night."

I cover my ears. "AHH." I so don't want to hear that. Aiden is completely pale and horrified. We all pretend that we didn't hear those words come out of his mouth. Some things are better off forgotten.

Aiden shakes his head and walks into the kitchen, and I take out the ultrasound pictures and show Laurie the babies.

"Can I have one?" she asks.

"Yes." I tear one off for her, and tears are in her eyes. "Are you okay, Laurie?" I ask her as Walker leaves the room.

She nods and wipes her eyes. "I'm just happy. He is amazing and he treats me so well. You're so used to doing everything alone, and then someone comes along flipping your world upside down. I love him."

I pull her into a hug. I can understand where she is coming from on certain levels. She raised Aiden all alone, sometimes working three jobs, and now Walker is here, taking care of her.

"You deserve to be happy." I lean back and wipe away the rest of her tears.

I hear Reid crying from his playpen, and I walk over and pick him up. "Did my boy miss me?" I rub his back, rocking him side to side.

He stops crying and rests his head on my chest. "Are you tired, huh?" I put his pacifier in his mouth and sit down on the couch, rocking him to sleep. Aiden sits down on the couch next to me, pulling both me and Reid against one side with Leah on the other.

We all snuggle on the couch watching TV. Laurie and Walker take the love seat. I love this. I love the little moments. They mean the most in the end. These are the things you remember. I'm going to remember Reid snuggling against my chest. Leah running to Aiden, so happy and carefree.

The moment I found out that I was pregnant, the look on his face, and the way I felt. Every single bit of it will stay in my mind forever.

Aiden

It's time for me to put an end to it. It's time for me to put him in the ground, making him pay for his sins.

He is home. I can see him sitting on the fucking couch like he doesn't have a worry in the world. Little does he know I am right outside his trailer. I have the guys standing all around me.

I know his play, when she was younger, was to try to scare her.

I am shaking. The anger I feel is something I cannot put into words. I've held her as she sobbed into my chest, telling me what he did to her, the horrible fucking things.

She is so strong; she went through so much and she is still smiling. She is beautiful; her heart is beautiful.

She knew what I am doing tonight. She kissed me and sent me on my way. This is for her.

I walk down the small hill and bust down the front door. I am not going to put a bullet in his head and call it good. Oh no, this is going to happen a different way.

He jumps up, turning off the TV. He is in underwear and a stained white T-shirt.

"What are you guys doing here?" he screeches. I want to tear out his fucking tongue so I don't have to hear another word coming out of that mouth of his. My stomach burns with anger, and the longer I look at him the worse it gets. "You're coming with me."

The prospects grip his arms and drag him out of the house. Logan hands me the gasoline, and I pour it in the hallway.

I come to a bedroom, and my hands are shaking as I open the

door. It's a little girl's room. I walk over to her dresser and open the drawer. I see a piece of paper, torn and brown from age.

Everything just hurts.

I lie in my bed every night and pray that I am rescued, that one night I can sleep without the fear of being woken up by him.

I am so scared. I am ten years old. What can I do?

It's getting worse. My stomach hurts because I haven't been allowed to eat in two days.

He laughs as he eats food in front of me, but I don't care. Maybe if I die, then I won't have to suffer again.

I'd rather not have food than him touch me again.

My wishes are never answered. He's done it over and over again for as long as I can remember.

It's like I'm dead inside. I'm numb to anything anymore. I stare at the mold crawling up the walls in my bedroom. Maybe that will take me out?

I hold onto the hope that one day everything will be better. I won't be here forever.

I think of the days when I will have peace.

To the future Gracelyn, I can't wait for you.

That just fucking tears my heart into pieces. With shaking hands, I set it down on the dresser. I am burning down all the shit in this house.

This is a new beginning; I am fucking killing all of her demons.

I walk into the room and take great pleasure in seeing him hanging from the ceiling. I have waited for this day for months.

He looks rough. I know it's been fucking with him that I haven't come for him until now.

"How's your brother?" I gloat.

He glares at me.

"That doesn't fucking scare me. You're just a big pussy. You have to hurt little girls to feel powerful." I grip his throat, wanting nothing more than to tear his throat out.

His eyes widen. I think it's finally sinking in that there's no getting out of this one.

I walk over to the wall of hell and take down some steel knuckles; then I stand in front of him. "You're going to die today. It's going to be fucking hell. Don't even bother begging because you're not getting out of this."

His arms are shaking above his head, and his eyes are clenched shut.

"LOOK AT ME!" I roar.

His eyes snap open.

"That's what you used to say to her, isn't it?" I ask him, vomit crawling up my throat at the sight of him.

"I'm sorry," he manages to get out through his trembling mouth.

What do I do? I laugh. "What the fuck am I going to do with that? You raped my woman, the mother of my kids, for YEARS! You think I will let that go?" I punch him hard in the face. I hear a crack and his jaw hangs loosely.

"Talk now, fucker." I smack his broken jawbone.

He screams and I laugh. I may look fucking crazy, but I can taste it. Revenge. I hit him over and over, until his face is unrecognizable. He leans over and spits out blood.

Logan hands me a pair of pliers, and I take his hand and pull out his fingernails slowly one at time.

"I bet you're feeling a little cold aren't you?" I take the acid off the ground and pour it over his head.

He shakes all over as the liquid runs all the way down to his feet. He shakes his head and hair falls to the floor. I let him stand there in agony for two hours, watching as he wakes up and passes out over and over again from the pain. I don't feel one ounce of regret. The only fucking thing I hate right now is being away from my family. I take the gun off the counter. "Look at me." I demand as I step in front of him.

He manages to get his eyes open.

"I want to be the last thing you see before you reach hell." I put the gun to his head and pull the trigger. His head flies back and he slumps over. The prospects take him down and drag him to the back of the property, where the hole is already dug.

They lay him next to the hole, and I look down at his body. If you can even call it that.

"May you rest in pieces, fucker." I kick him into the hole.

I stare at him and feel peace; I feel peace for her. For the rest of her life, she can know that he is gone and she will never see him again.

I take out my gun and shoot him again for good measure, as the prospects cover him with dirt.

I stay until he is completely buried. "I hope you enjoy hell." I turn my back to the grave and walk to my bike. I just want to go home.

The moment I pull up, she opens the door for me. When I step inside the house, she wraps her arms around me.

I hold her, kissing the top of her head. "You okay?"

She pulls back and looks at me, her eyes filled with tears. "Is it over?" she asks, like she is afraid.

I cup her face. "It's over. He is dead."

She nods, resting her head on my chest. "It's like I can breathe fully for the first time."

"I love you."

She leans up and kisses me. "And I love you."

EPILOGUE

GRACE

THE GRIM SINNER'S MOTORYCYCLE CLUB

A few weeks later

I AM FEEDING REID HIS LUNCH, HIS BEAUTIFUL BLUE EYES STARING at me. "Open wide." I move the spoon toward his mouth.

He doesn't move but continues to stare at me. I set the spoon down, getting kind of scared.

Just as I am about to take him out of the high chair, he grins and smacks the tray. "Ma ma ma ma."

My heart stops. The waterworks happen, and there's no stopping them. I lift him out of his seat and hug him.

My heart is so full.

Aiden

I watch from the door as they have this moment together. She has changed a lot over the past couple of weeks. She is lighter and happier, and it's like she laughed fully and completely for the first time.

I don't think she realized how much of a burden it was having him alive until he was gone. All the anxiety and stress has slowly melted away.

I love her more every single day. I didn't think that was possible, but I do. The way she takes care of Leah and Reid is the sexiest thing I have seen.

She loves with her whole heart, and I am happy to have a part of that. I back away from the door, smiling, and let her have her moment.

Seven months later

If anybody ever says that pregnancy is easy, they're lying. I am pregnant with two babies instead of one and, on top of that, it's hotter than Satan's balls outside.

Reid is one year old now, and Leah is changing before my eyes every single day. She is sassy—she puts all the MC guys in their place. Aiden thinks it's the most hilarious thing.

On top of playing softball, she is in karate. Her words were, "You can't always rely on a weapon. I want to *be* the weapon." Aiden was floating on air; he signed her up the very next day.

Reid has turned into a complete momma's boy. He wants me to hold him all the time—not that I mind. He is crawling all over the place. We had to baby proof everything.

It's been very peaceful. The drug problem has been completely eradicated.

We are currently at a barbecue at the club. I shift Reid higher on my hip and wobble over to the food table—just as I feel something wet fall down my leg.

I look up at the person in front of me, and it's Travis. His eyes are on my legs. He points at my legs before running to Aiden.

That's when the contraction hits. I grip the table and grit my teeth, waiting for it to pass. Through the pain of my contraction, I hear yelling and feet pounding toward me. "Gracie." Aiden wraps his arm around me, and Laurie takes Reid.

"My water broke."

His eyes widen and he looks down at my stomach, like the babies' heads are just going to pop out and say peek a boo! He bends over and picks me up bridal style.

"I can walk, Aiden," I tell him and he shakes his head furiously.

Leah runs over to us. "Is it finally time?" she asks, her eyes lit with happiness.

"Yes." I touch her face and she runs off, yelling for Tiffany that her brothers are coming.

Oh, did I mention that I am having twin boys? Leah is in for it for sure with three brothers.

Logan opens Aiden's truck door and sets me inside. I grip his hand, not allowing him to leave just yet. "Let's do this," I whisper, feeling kind of overwhelmed that this is actually happening.

He cups my jaw. "Let's meet our boys." He kisses me so tenderly that I want to cry. I can feel so much love and emotion in that kiss.

～

A forever amount of hours later

AIDEN IS LYING in bed with me. I have one baby on my chest, and Aiden has the other.

Meet Alex and Jacob; they are identical twins. I can tell them apart because Alex has bigger ears.

"I am so tired," I confess. The labor was hell.

"Go to sleep, sweetheart. You did so amazing. I am so proud of you." He kisses me and smooths my hair out of my face.

I feel like I am a hundred feet tall at his compliment. I close my eyes and rest my head on his shoulder.

Aiden takes Alex from me and holds him against his chest too. I turn over slightly, resting my hands against my babies.

"We are so blessed, Aiden." I rub the back of Jacob's head.

"Thank you for giving me this beautiful life," he tells me. I just fell more in love with him.

All my dreams are coming true. Wait, no. They have come true, and it's way better than I ever expected.

I fall asleep with everything right in the world—with my babies and Aiden.

Grace
Leah 16

"What the fuck are you saying, Leah?" Aiden growls, standing up from the couch. Leah is holding her own against Aiden because she wants to go on her first date.

"Dad, please. He will be here soon," she pleads, giving him her puppy eyes.

Jacob, Reid, Alex, and I are silently laughing on the couch. I know this is Aiden's worst nightmare come true.

Reid, Jacob, and Alex are glued to each other at the hip, and they are always getting into trouble.

Aiden closes his eyes, trying to compose himself. "What the fuck do you mean he will be here soon?"

Leah nods her head slowly. "He will be here soon. Please, Dad." She folds her hands in front of her chest.

His eyes narrow on her like he is daring her to say another word. I hear a beep on the wall letting us know someone's at the gate.

Her eyes widen, and she makes a run for the keypad on the

wall. Aiden tries to catch her, but she pushes the button before he can reach her.

"Leah!" he yells and I burst out laughing, not able to help myself anymore.

Aiden glares at me, eye twitching, which doesn't faze me one bit.

That's when I hear the motorcycle. I laugh louder and look out the window to see it pull up in front of the house. I rub Aubree's back, and she laughs at everyone like she knows what is happening. She is two.

Aubree is our daughter. We adopted her a few months ago, and we've all fallen in love with her. Aiden and I missed our kids being young, so we decided to open our home to another precious baby.

Aiden gives Leah a look that would surely scare a grown man, but not Leah. We all know he is really just a huge softy.

"You better not tell me that he is on his motorcycle and expects you to get on the back of it," Aiden says in a voice that is completely calm.

Leah's eyes widen in an *oh shit* look. Aiden tears open the door, and we all run outside after him after I put Aubree in her play pen. Aiden stalks down to the guy on the motorcycle, and I hold my breath waiting for him to take off his helmet. I burst out laughing when I see it's Benjamin who is her friend.

Leah smirks. "Gotcha, Dad." Aiden holds his heart like he is about to have a heart attack. Aiden is terrified at the thought of her dating.

Then my boys yell, "Look out!" They have somehow magically gotten roman candles and lit them. I run for the house as they all start shooting fireworks at each other.

I turn southern mom in a split second. "If you don't stop, I'm going to whoop y'alls asses!" Aiden is glaring at the boys, who have done a great job of ignoring him, and Leah is hiding out behind a bush. I don't know how they got them. I threw them away a week ago, but the boys must have hidden more of them.

Once the roman candles burn out, I step out of the house with my arms across my chest. One by one, they all turn to look at me, pale. Reid tries to wiggle his way out of it. "Mom, these were the last ones."

I don't say a word but point toward the house. They slowly make their way inside with their heads hanging down, trying to make me feel sorry for them. Leah runs after them, trying to avoid Aiden at all costs. I have to give her props. It was a good prank. Aiden is extremely protective over her, and she knew he'd freak out if she had a date.

Leah can handle herself though. She has been in MMA for months, and I will not be surprised if, after college, she does it professionally. She still loves softball but she really loves MMA.

Benjamin slowly backs out of the driveway, Aiden glares at him the whole time. Benjamin is a eighteen-year-old prospect at the club.

I sit down on the step, and Aiden walks over and joins me. We look at each other, bursting out laughing. "Our fucking kids, man." Aiden says like he is so tired.

"I wouldn't have it any other way." I lay my head on his shoulder, looking up at the stars.

Yeah, everything is just perfect.

The END
For now

AUTHOR NOTE

Author Note:

I HAVE CONTEMPLATED MANY TIMES WHETHER I SHOULD WRITE THIS, because this book has been so hard for me. This book is fiction, but Grace's childhood is based on a true story.

Whose story you may ask?

Mine.

Grace's childhood was so very real because I lived it—her dad was my dad. Her uncle was my uncle.

I could have written a book that was all flowers and daisies, but that's not real life. I wanted to share this with you guys to show that there is hope at the end of it all.

I was terrified, but I felt the urge to let you guys know that Grace is me. It's so empowering to do this, but at the same time it's so scary.

Because I have gone from fewer than five people knowing to sharing it with thousands upon thousands of people.

It's so freeing; it's like a burden has been lifted off my chest. Having a voice is powerful, and I want to use my platform to share my story.

I want those who have suffered in any way, shape, or form know you're not alone. Tomorrow is a new day. It won't always be shitty. I promise.

You have this! <3

Thank you all so, so, so much for being a part of my journey and my healing process. This has set my demons free. I thank you for that.

PS: It was really amazing killing off certain characters in this book. ;)

ABOUT THE AUTHOR

Author Links
Page: https://www.facebook.com/Author-Teagan-Wilde-2112786585717655/
Facebook Reader Group:
https://www.facebook.com/groups/1163716090445778/
My email is: authorleannashers@gmail.com (Feel free to email me! I love to hear your thoughts!)

My Social Media's under LeAnn Ashers
Facebook: https://www.facebook.com/LeAnnashers
Instagram: https://www.instagram.com/leann_ashers/
Twitter: https://twitter.com/LeannAshers
Goodreads:
https://www.goodreads.com/author/show/14733196.LeAnn_Ashers

WANT MORE TO READ?

HERE IS MY OTHER WORKS!

Forever Series
Protecting His Forever
Loving His Forever

Devil Souls MC Series
Torch
Techy
Butcher
Liam

GRIM SINNERS MC SERIES

LANE

Wilder
Smiley
Travis

This series is under my paranormal pen name
Teagan Wilde

Raleigh Texas Wolves
Damon